G R JORDAN

Antisocial Behaviour

A Highlands and Islands Detective Thriller

First edition

ISBN: 978-1-915562-04-3

This book was professionally typeset on Reedsy.
Find out more at reedsy.com

Children say they are unhappy in every language they have. They say it in silence, and they say it in riots.

JAY GRIFFITHS

Contents

Foreword

This novel is set around the highlands and islands of Scotland and while using the area and its people as an inspiration, the specific places and persons in this book are entirely fictitious. The two Inverness estates featured in the book are entirely fictitious.

Acknowledgement

To Ken, Jessica, Jean, Colin and Rosemary for your work in bringing this novel to completion, your time and effort is deeply appreciated.

Novels by G R Jordan

The Highlands and Islands Detective series (Crime)

1. Water's Edge
2. The Bothy
3. The Horror Weekend
4. The Small Ferry
5. Dead at Third Man
6. The Pirate Club
7. A Personal Agenda
8. A Just Punishment
9. The Numerous Deaths of Santa Claus
10. Our Gated Community
11. The Satchel
12. Culhwch Alpha
13. Fair Market Value
14. The Coach Bomber
15. The Culling at Singing Sands
16. Where Justice Fails
17. The Cortado Club
18. Cleared to Die
19. Man Overboard!
20. Antisocial Behaviour
21. Rogues' Gallery

Kirsten Stewart Thrillers (Thriller)

1. A Shot at Democracy
2. The Hunted Child
3. The Express Wishes of Mr MacIver
4. The Nationalist Express
5. The Hunt for 'Red Anna'
6. The Execution of Celebrity
7. The Man Everyone Wanted
8. Busman's Holiday

The Contessa Munroe Mysteries (Cozy Mystery)

1. Corpse Reviver
2. Frostbite
3. Cobra's Fang

The Patrick Smythe Series (Crime)

1. The Disappearance of Russell Hadleigh
2. The Graves of Calgary Bay
3. The Fairy Pools Gathering

Austerley & Kirkgordon Series (Fantasy)

1. Crescendo!
2. The Darkness at Dillingham
3. Dagon's Revenge

4. Ship of Doom

Supernatural and Elder Threat Assessment Agency (SETAA)
Series (Fantasy)

1. Scarlett O'Meara: Beastmaster

Island Adventures Series (Cosy Fantasy Adventure)

1. Surface Tensions

Dark Wen Series (Horror Fantasy)

1. The Blasphemous Welcome
2. The Demon's Chalice

Chapter 01

Peter watched the child on the swing glaring at him. The little brats had always been cheeky to them, didn't know their place, and it was about time somebody took some action on that. They weren't even part of a gang; they just came along here to this play park, the one that Peter and his friends operated from, and just expected to take it over. It was after eight o'clock at night, everyone knew this is where Peter's gang hung out, and nobody else got to use it. He didn't care that the kid had only just left primary school. Apparently, he'd been a real pain there, too.

Peter watched the kid swinging back and forward, laughing at his mates and then, he laughed over at Peter. Beside Peter, three of his own mates were laughing, throwing things at each other, and drinking down the red liquid they had purchased from the off licence around the corner. They may only have been fifteen, but they could pass for eighteen if they wanted.

Not that it mattered once Davey was working. Davey was Greg's older brother and he passed them alcohol anytime they wanted it, the good stuff as well, not just a crappy tin of lager or a beer. Instead, it was proper stuff that got you properly smashed.

Peter dragged on a cigarette, then put it to the ground. It was after eight; these kids needed to move on.

'Oi, Jamesy, let's get these wee glyps out of here.'

'You're right. What are they doing here? Anyway, look; there's Jen.'

Peter looked over and saw Jenny arriving, black jacket around her shoulders, but in the straight cut-off jeans. Peter liked her legs, and he liked Jenny as a whole. She sat and drank with the boys and Peter hoped that one day soon she'd do a lot more than that with him. She had an older sister and, according to some of the other lads, she was good for it. She had taste though. You had to be doing well in the gang; you had to be up there for she only knocked about with those at the top.

Peter was doing all right. He'd stolen a few things, got into a number of fights, and come out on top because he was a pretty big lad for his age. He'd also managed to acquire a number of knives. But if some of the other guys got here and found they were sharing the park at this time of night with those little kids, he'd be a laughingstock.

He waited until Jenny came over, put his arm around her and watched as she looked up at him.

'You got anything?' she asked. He produced a bottle and handed it to her and watched as her lips took a slug of the red liquid. When she put the bottle back down, she looked at him, 'When I said have you got anything, I meant anything good.'

Peter didn't. He hadn't been heavily into drugs, only popped the odd pill. He cursed himself. Knowing that Jenny would have been here tonight, he should have had something on him.

'Just give us a minute, Jenny. Need to shift these brats on. Come on, Jamesy.' The pair marched over to the swings.

The play park was smack in the middle of the housing estate, one that had seen better days. However, it was not run down to the extent where people had actually left, but instead there was a thriving drug culture, supply and demand, running underneath the mundane every day.

Several residents had tried unsuccessfully to curb such activities. Peter knew many of the guys who dealt; he'd even bought from the odd one. This was the space for it and those guys had left the likes of Peter and his gang to make sure that the place was clear, available to operate in and not crammed up with pesky kids and their mums and dads who would follow. They just wanted the older ones, the ones who could find a bit of money or even steal something to get a fix.

'Oi, squirt, beat it,' said Peter to the nearest kid. Dressed in a bomber jacket, the kid looked up, gave him a snarl and went back to swinging, laughing with his mates.

'I said beat it. Go on; piss off.'

The kid turned and glared at him. There must have been at least three years between them, but still the kid felt it necessary to give some cheek back. 'It's an open country. You don't have to do anything; the much nicer swing is yours.'

'I told you to piss off,' said Peter, and reached inside his jacket, pulling out a butterfly knife from inside. He opened it up and stepped towards the kid who he could now see was beginning to panic. The mates around the child had disappeared, leaving him on the swing with Peter pointing the knife at him. Taking it up to the kid's face, he grabbed him by the hair and pressed the knife up to his throat.

Peter could hear Jenny coming over and he turned, giving her a smile, 'Look at this, Jen, he's crapping it.'

The young kid had been so eager to have a go at Peter and

3

suddenly wasn't saying anything. Peter could see the kid beginning to urinate, scared stiff with the knife at his throat. Peter yanked his hair. 'Go on, piss off,' he said, throwing the child down onto the floor. He wrapped his arm around Jen, 'Hey,' he said, and planted a kiss on her lips. They were out in front of everyone, and together the two of them brazenly fondled each other. The rest of the gang laughed and jeered, and they returned back to the red liquid from the bottle.

It was about one in the morning when Peter left the playground, having seen some of the older kids from the gang. There'd been plenty of laughing and joking and he had spent a large part of the night with Jenny, boasting of how he'd sent a little kid packing. Some of the older ones got a bit annoyed with him and a fight had kicked off between Jamesy and someone else new to the gang, ending up in a bloody nose for Jamesy. They wrecked the roundabout as well just for fun, hitting it with hammers, but it was time to head back.

Peter waved goodbye to Jamesy not far from the play park and walked down the alley which was a shortcut through to the block of flats where he lived. As he got towards the end of the alley, he thought he heard something and turned around, but there was no one there. The rain had started to fall, small pitter-patters, and Peter pulled up his hoodie, covering his face, put his hands in his pockets and went to trudge home.

As he turned, he saw a pair of feet in front of him. He went to grab the stalker, but he was grabbed by the throat, taken off his feet and driven against the wall. Before he could say or do anything, he felt something ripping into his gut once, then twice, then a third time. The word 'scumbag' was the last he heard as the knife continued to plunge into him. The pain was immense, but he didn't black out, instead, feeling every blow dealt.

* * *

The car went round and round, crashing off the occasional bollard; he then steered it into the car park of the supermarket, ramming it into some loose trolleys that had been left lying around. He laughed, wondering why they didn't do the supermarket more often.

It was three in the morning and beside him sat Patty, who looked delighted at his driving. In the back, Amy was huddled up with Derek and part of Johnny wanted to pull over so he could get down to some serious necking as well. Patty was enjoying this. She'd driven Johnny around the estate several times, having stolen cars and boasted about it. There would only be another year or two before she too would be able to drive legally.

She wanted a big Merc, but Johnny wanted something faster. He was only fourteen but did pretty much as he wanted. No doubt his mother was lying in some alcoholic stupor up in the flat, whereas he was out enjoying himself. Patty had been good to find. She had the looks, but she also had the hands. His second girlfriend, and she knew much more about things than the first had, a timid, shy girl.

As he turned the car around, and drove at full speed over a couple of speed bumps, they heard the suspension angrily kick back at the manoeuvre. Patty urged him on and he drove like a wild thing in and out of the retail park's car spaces, hitting corners at full pelt until the car slid out and crashed, causing their backseat occupants to shout.

'Take it easy,' said one. 'Trying to do stuff back here.'

'Piss off,' said Johnny. 'Time to drive; time for that later.' He looked over at Patty and nodded. Patty's father worked night shift and so his flat would be there for them. While it was dark, it was best to drive around in the cars. You couldn't get away with it in the daytime.

'Let's try the street,' said Patty

'No way,' said Amy. 'In and out of there? People will go daft.'

'Exactly,' said Patty, 'but we can get through, drive around, cause havoc and get out. Then we can ditch this car afterwards.'

'You're crazy,' said Johnny.

'Not as crazy as your driving,' said Patty, and she reached over and gave Johnny a long, deep kiss. 'Bloody gorgeous you are. Do you know that?' she said.

Johnny felt warm inside. He'd show her, all right. He dropped the handbrake, racing off as fast as he could but came up to a small roundabout. The car hit the curb, but Johnny managed to hang onto the car as they tore down a residential street in front of a block of flats. This is where Patty lived, her little kingdom, and he was going to show his queen a good time on her doorstep.

Patty pressed the horn, blaring through the night as Johnny raced along. She pointed to the path at the side, and he spun off up the pavement onto the path which ran round and then underneath the block of flats. Patty blared the horn again. Johnny lost control, the car careering through several bedding plants, muck sent spiralling into the air.

'Bloody hell,' said Patty. 'Nice one. Come on.'

Johnny kept it going, spinning the car back around and driving deliberately through all the flower beds. There were shouts from windows, barely audible to them above the noise the car was making. Then lights were coming on.

'One more time,' said Patty, 'one more time. We'll show them.' She rolled down the window, put her arm out, and put two fingers up to the air. 'Everyone,' she said, 'come on.'

As she looked behind, the rear window was being put down, the two-finger salute coming from all corners of the car. Johnny obliged as well, one hand on the steering wheel and then struggled as they hit the curb and crashed into another car.

'Bollocks,' he said.

'Just reverse it,' said Patty, 'just reverse it.'

But Johnny always knew what to do. She put her hand over the top of his, as he adjusted the gearstick and he raced the car backwards and then spun it, pointing out to the main road again. The car careered down off the pavement, tore along, and they raced just over a half a mile away, stopping at a small lay-by hidden from the main road by a mass of trees.

'You're wicked,' said Patty, reaching over and beginning to kiss Johnny. 'I think it's time we headed back to my place.'

Johnny looked up. She had those eyes, and he was trouble. Wonderful trouble.

'Do we just ditch it here?' asked Johnny.

'No,' said Patty, 'we'll do it elsewhere.'

Johnny went to start the car again but looked up into the rear-view mirror and saw a pair of lights.

'There's a car just come in. Patty, who the hell's that? It's four in the morning.'

He watched Patty look out her window. Then she rolled it down and started giving the fingers.

'Looks like some old git,' she said, 'I can sort it.' She reached down into the well of the car and picked up a bottle of whisky, taking a large slug of it before handing it to Johnny. She didn't like whisky that much, happier when it was something that tasted better. But to keep him happy, she always drunk it when with him.

He looked up in the rear-view mirror. 'Patty, that person's coming over. Look.'

Patty leaned out of the window again. 'Go on, piss off,' she shouted. Johnny told her, 'That's it, Patty. You show them. We could crash the car into theirs. That would show them, wouldn't it?'

Patty turned around laughing. 'Yes.' As she did so, something came in through the window and landed right beside the gearstick of the car. The pair of them looked down at it. It was oval-shaped and almost in disbelief, they recognised it as a grenade.

'What the hell?' said Johnny, and then it exploded.

He felt like his body was being ripped apart, things puncturing it, and his head swam in pain and agony, but he didn't black out. Instead, something was keeping him alive. He couldn't move. Beside him, he saw the half-disappeared face of Patty. Then there was a shadow around the car.

There was someone there, with a large bottle of something, or maybe it was one of those canisters. They were pouring something. The canister appeared at the open window beside Patty's wrecked body. Liquid was poured in. The last thing Johnny saw was the flames rising up before his body shut down completely.

Chapter 02

Macleod rolled over in his bed as the telephone rang. This untimely call penetrating the senses at the early hours of the morning, it couldn't be good. If they had been able to delay by an hour or two, they'd have done it, allowed him to come in at a more civilized time, maybe even six.

His hand shot out onto the bedside table, went to grab the phone, fumbled it, and he heard it hitting the floor. Beside him, Jane rolled over until she was lying on top of him, one arm disappearing off the end of the bed, fumbling around for the phone. He heard her laugh before the phone was pushed up beside his ear, and she rolled back off him, giving him a gentle smack on the backside. It really wasn't the correct mood for answering a call like this.

'This is Macleod. What's up?'

'Sorry to bother you, Detective Inspector, but you're required at the station. We have two incidents, both believed to be murder in the Inverness area. If you could attend as soon as possible, be much appreciated.'

'You say two?'

'Yes, that's correct. There are two, one where a youth has

been stabbed to death, and another where a group of joy riders have been killed. We're not sure if it's murder, but the traffic branch have said that there is some doubt.'

'Okay,' said Macleod. 'Who have you called from my team?'

'Just you, Inspector. You're the one down for the on call.'

'That I am, but we've got two instances, and both sounding serious, so kindly call the rest of the team. Tell them I want to see them in the station in half an hour. In fact, make it forty-five minutes.'

As he closed the phone call, Jane, his partner, leaned across, whispering in his ear. 'Is that an extra fifteen minutes for me?'

'No,' said Macleod. 'That's fifteen minutes to get into the shower and wake up.'

'You weren't like this when we started out. You'd have forgone your fifteen minutes of shower.'

'You must be slipping,' said Macleod, hauling himself out of bed and dragging himself through to the shower room. He turned the water on, allowing it to soak into his bones as he stood with his back to the door. He put his face under the water, letting his eyes feel the heat, and then stretched out blindly with his right hand for the shower gel that should be over on the wall. He fumbled for it, but he couldn't find anything.

He felt a cool liquid going across his back, followed by a pair of hands, rubbing away at the tight knots in his shoulders. 'Slipping, am I?' said Jane.

'Fifteen minutes and out,' said Macleod. 'Just fifteen minutes.'

'Aye, you're right, Seoras,' said Jane. 'It's not really worth it.' He shook the water from his eyes and turn round to see her stepping back out of the shower. A hand reached out, pulling her back in. 'You're always worth it,' he said.

'And how corny is that? Remember, fifteen minutes.'

Detective Inspector Seoras Macleod was in a good mood twenty minutes later as he drove into Inverness and across the large bridge that separated the Black Isle from the city. The dawn was barely breaking the sky and he could still see the lights of the city beaming out from the shadows. To his right, he noted that the lifeboat was still in the marina.

One benefit that he noticed arriving at this time of the day was the roundabout by the football stadium. He found it to be devoid of cars and he was able to cruise past and on to the turn-off that would take him down to the police station. Getting in at this hour was clearly that much easier.

As he strolled into the main office, he noticed that the lights were on, and his constable, Alan Ross, was already at his desk.

'What have we got?' asked Macleod.

'Well, sir, we have a brutal stabbing, out on the Warmsley estate. A youth has been gutted with a knife. Meanwhile, on the Knockmalley estate, there's a car gone up, four youths in it, all burned to death by the looks of it. Traffic were out with it, though, and they don't think that it crashed. They believe it was set alight deliberately. Also unsure of some of the damage that's done to the car. They're saying it looks like it's come from the inside.'

'Inside? Not just a petrol tank explosion or something?' asked Macleod.

'Don't know yet. Had a call five minutes ago from Jona Nakamura. She's on her way over there.'

'Good,' said Macleod. 'Where's Hope?'

He heard the clip of small heels coming in behind him.

'I'm here, Seoras, all of about one minute behind you. What's

11

the deal?'

'Two murders,' he said. 'Or potentially two. I'll take the one that's definitely a murder. Looks like someone was stabbed to death, a youth out on the Walmsley estate. You and Ross get over to Knockmalley. There's a car burnt out over there, four people in it, but traffic is saying it doesn't look like it was an accident. They're thinking there might be something more suspicious. Jona's on her way over there now. I'll wait for Clarissa. She can come with me.'

'And Clarissa is here,' announced a voice and Macleod turned to see the tour de force that was his detective sergeant entering the room in tartan trousers, and boots up her knees. There was a long shawl wrapped around her as usual, with a large brooch keeping it in place. Today's hair colour was purple, and she gave Macleod a grin as she approached.

'You and I is it, Seoras?'

'You may accompany me to the scene of a murder,' said Macleod, determined not to give the woman a smile.

Clarissa turned to Hope. 'You see? I told you. He's liking me over you.'

Macleod went to respond and then thought better of it. 'Time to get a move on,' he said. 'You know what these estates are like. Be prepared for a bit of trouble. Make sure we talk to uniform, and give them every assistance to keep a calm scene.'

'Will do, Seoras,' said Hope, turning on her heel and giving Ross a wave.

'Should we take my car?' asked Clarissa.

'No,' said Macleod. 'Probably better if I drive. These estates, they don't take to classic numbers like your own car. You've got to be careful in case they get a bit rough with it. Might get the odd key scrape.'

12

'Really?' said Clarissa. 'It's the car and not my driving you're worried about?'

'Of course,' said Macleod, pulling his jacket around him. 'Let's go.' He left Clarissa in his wake, smiling to himself that at least they were going in his car.

* * *

Macleod stood looking at the body in front of him and the multiple knife wounds that it had suffered. The area was covered in blood and Jona Nakamura's deputy was standing close by, waiting for the inspector to finish with the scene before she took the body away.

'How quick do you think he died?' asked Macleod.

'Not quick enough,' said Mercy Johnson. The woman's dark skin stood out against the white coverall outfit and Macleod thought that her eyes, deep set on her face, made her look wise beyond her years.

'What do you mean by that?' asked Macleod.

'What I mean is, he'd have felt every single one of those knife wounds going in, unless shock killed him, which I don't believe it did. He'd have bled out.'

'So, he'd have got a close look at his killer then?'

'Indeed, he would,' said Mercy, 'But by the looks of it, he didn't put up much of a struggle.'

'Too weak or too slow?' asked Macleod.

'Too slow? I mean he's a male youth, probably heading towards sixteen or seventeen. He's not going to be lacking in strength. That being said, a strong man could have held him, but there's no indication he's been held. If you look at the wrist, there's no marks. Instead, there's just countless knife wounds.'

'Countless?' said Macleod.

'Sorry,' said Mercy, 'Uncounted. I still have to do that.' Macleod nodded, turned around to Clarissa, who'd been gathering some information for him.

'Who is it?' asked Macleod.

'Peter Olive. Lives on the estate. Last seen at the play park not far from here. Tended to hang out there most of the time but has got links to various drug dealers, although not believed to be dealing himself. Bit of a hard man within a gang, at least that's what they're saying.'

'Who's saying?'

'Some of the other kids around here. Seems the whole estate's nearly up.'

'Has he got any parents?'

'Yes,' said Clarissa, 'They're certainly up. We got his parents and we've got a lot of other parents as well.' Macleod heard a shout from behind him.

'Where's my boy? Where is my boy?'

Macleod turned to see a woman being forcibly held back by a couple of uniformed police officers. They weren't laying down the law with her, just simply keeping her back from the scene.

'Clarissa, go and give a hand. I'll be along directly,' said Macleod. Clarissa gave a nod and turned to walk directly to the woman while Macleod took another look at the scene.

There'd been no attempt to hide what had happened. If anything, it was as if the killer had been quick about this and made sure it happened somewhere fairly public. The body wasn't hidden behind dust bins in some remote alley. It was quite possible that someone would walk along here through this thoroughfare. Macleod looked up and couldn't see any cameras. Sometimes in these estates, you had them, but not here in this spot, and it told him that somebody had premeditated this.

'What sort of blade are we talking?' Macleod asked Mercy.

'At the moment, I'm saying it's a good eight inches. That's just a guess, probably serrated edge. It was not something from a kitchen. It's a proper weapon.'

'Any weapons on our friend here?'

'There's a butterfly knife that he never got deployed,' said Mercy, 'inside his jacket.'

'Okay, Mercy. I'm done. Thank you very much. I'll speak to you back at the station. If you need anything, give me a shout.'

'Will do, Inspector. I think Jona is intending to come over once I get back and I've gone through everything with her.'

'Make sure you cross-reference this with the scene she's at currently.'

'Of course, Inspector, but are you sure? The other one's a car fire.'

'It's a car fire that happened quite soon after this one, and not that far away. May be retaliation. Just keep it in mind.'

Macleod turned around and walked towards the police cordon that was holding crowds back from the scene. As he approached, he saw Clarissa off to one side with a woman who was weeping bitterly. However, around her had formed a small crowd of other women who seemed to be shouting at her.

'Excuse me,' said Macleod, 'what's going on here?'

'I'm just going through some questions, Inspector, with Mrs Olive. These other ladies seem to be having an input. I've asked them to step away.'

'We're not going anywhere. It's good to see him dead,' said a voice.

'Who are you?' asked Macleod, drawing himself up to his full height and standing in front of the woman.

'Mary, Mary Thorpe and I know who you are. You want to be looking at that guy there, not for his killer. Somebody did us a favour. He's into drugs, that one. Spreading drugs, bullying other kids, causing misery.'

'My boy is dead,' said Mrs Olive, standing up straight and turning on the woman, 'You hear me? I bet you it was your husband that did it. Bet you were all involved.' Suddenly, the woman was swinging, looking to attack them and Clarissa stepped in between. She pulled the woman to one side.

'Clarissa, move to the Incident Room now. I'll cover the rest of this.'

Clarissa marched Mrs Olive off to the temporary van that had arrived on scene and Macleod turned round to the women that were now gathered around him. Over their shoulders, he saw some men arriving.

'That's enough,' said Macleod, 'I've got a dead boy on my hands. What he is, was, or whatever is what I'd like to find out and you'll have plenty of opportunity to tell me, but not like this. I'm going to take the names of each and every one of you and I'll interview you and you can talk to me about what he was like.'

'I'll tell you what he was like,' said Mary Thorpe, 'up to no good. Threatened my wee one several times. That play park's a no-go area for the kids that need it and all the drugs are running through there. His sort are all acting up like they're big men. They walk round here after five at night and they're shouting at you and they're coming after you. Jane over there

16

had her pram taken off her. Run off with it, dumped it in the river. Just about had the baby out of it by the time they took it.'

Macleod held up his hands, 'Okay, that may be accurate, and I want to know more about it because somebody's just come along and murdered that boy behind me. You may think it was the best thing for him. You may even be right, but it's a murder, which I intend to solve. As for your kids, clearly, somebody is quite happy with dispatching people of this age, so I'd keep them indoors. Now, it's nearly five in the morning. Kindly disperse and let my team get on with what they're doing.'

'Just make sure you take them down as well,' said Mary Thorpe. 'Just make sure that they pay for what they're doing.'

'I'll be looking at all things,' said Macleod. 'Now go on, home, please.'

A hand went on Mary Thorpe's shoulder. 'He's right,' said a man. 'Come on. Nothing left to do here. The piece of rubbish is dead.'

Macleod watched the people disperse, slowly and with much chatter between them. He had the unenviable task now of talking to a mother whose child had just died, and he wasn't looking forward to it. He also knew he shouldn't leave Clarissa in there too much longer. She'd need support as well. In some ways, it was easier when the nice ones died because there were rarely many people who had a reason for killing them. The trouble with somebody like this was there were too many suspects.

17

Chapter 3

Hope McGrath looked at the shell of a vehicle that was left, the fire now extinguished by the firemen who had been on scene so rapidly. They were just withdrawing, now convinced that the vehicle was no longer a danger to reignite, and the scene was fully handed over to the police. Jona Nakamura was quickly in and amongst it while Hope stood surveying her work. She arrived on scene with Alan Ross who had met up with their uniform colleagues and helped with the organisation of interviews with the nearby crowd. He was just returning from the initial conversations, and Hope saw that he didn't have much of a bounce in his step.

'You look a bit dire.'

'Well, there's a crime scene,' said Alan. 'You don't get to walk around with a big smile on your face.'

'No, and you haven't got that glitter in your eye either,' said Hope. 'What's up?'

'Nobody saw it. Nobody saw it happen but according to traffic, potentially, there was another car here. I scanned everywhere for a CCTV and there isn't any.'

'Do we still think it didn't just go on fire on them? It wasn't a mistake?'

'You're best talking to Jona about that,' said Alan. 'I see she's knee-deep as ever in the evidence.'

They both looked over and caught Jona's eye as she sifted through the vehicle. She put up a hand, indicating they should wait for a moment. Thirty seconds later, she stepped out of the vehicle and walked over towards Hope.

'What's up?' asked Hope.

'Well, for one, this is murder. I believe there are the remains of a grenade inside of that car. I've got shrapnel lodged inside the doors, and I think if I scan the area, we'll probably pick up a bit more. The glass is obviously broken out of all the windows, but that, of course, could have been from the heat of the fire.'

'A grenade?' said Hope. 'So, what? Somebody threw a grenade into the car?'

'Either that or they were dumb enough to have one in with them and pulled the pin out,' said Jona. 'That seems a highly unlikely scenario, however, especially as the car was then doused in some sort of fuel and set alight. That much I can tell or at least suspect. I think very much this is a murder. Traffic picked up some markings on the floor for a second car. It was quite close in. How long did it stop for, who knows? Whether it was here when the grenade went off, again, who knows but we haven't had any reports of a car with its windows blown out. I'm suspecting it was the delivery mechanism for the grenade.'

'The people inside, anything about them?' asked Hope.

'Well, I've only just got a look. However, they are all young. Youths, four of them, maybe just about coming up to the age when you could legally drive. That's only from a rough height and size. That sort of age, you never know.'

'I've got the constable sweeping the area at the moment trying to see if we can get any idea who was in the car,' said

Ross. 'I've asked them to keep a tight cordon around the area. We could have a number of parents on our doorstep here looking for children.'

'Good one. Okay. Go see what else you can find.'

Hope took a walk around the car, keeping her distance at the moment. By the look of it, it was fairly souped-up. Probably they had stolen it from a better class of area than this. That was the idea around here, wasn't it? Grab something, drive off in it, set it on fire, or dump it down a ditch. Hope knew there'd been numerous problems on the Knockmalley estate, one that her colleagues in uniform were struggling to get a handle on. She didn't blame them. There seemed to be so much going on, as well as several drug operators in the area. Knife crime had gone up. Fortunately, they hadn't seen much of weapons, but this was a grenade.

Could it be that they were involved in the drugs and not simply joy riders but actually were mules for the drug dealers? Did somebody decide that they were on the wrong patch? All these thoughts swept over Hope. She picked up her phone to call Macleod, but the call wouldn't go through. It got closed off when the answering machine kicked in.

'Seoras, it's me,' said Hope to the answering machine. 'As feared, we have a murder of four youths over here killed by a grenade into the car, the car then set alight. I'm struggling to understand quite what's going on, whether these are simply joy riders or whether they're involved in any drugs. Alan's got a constable sweeping the area interviewing anyone we can find, but so far we haven't had anyone come up to say they've seen what's going on.'

'Detective Sergeant.'

'That's me,' said Hope, turning to see a man close by holding out his hand.

'Sergeant Hooper,' he said, 'traffic. I just thought that I'd bring you up to date because clearly, this is going to be handed over to you and not coming with us.'

'Thank you,' said Hope. 'Jona said you've identified a second vehicle.'

'Well, there's some tread indicating a vehicle pulled up at speed beside the victim's vehicle. We're not sure if there were any shenanigans before that. What I can say is that that car didn't crash and then go alight.'

'Jona has confirmed that,' said Hope. 'She said it was set alight, fuel of some sort doused in.'

'Exactly. Look, I'll send over the tyre prints and the rest to Jona. I'll also send you a copy of what we find, but to be honest there's not much else we can do for you.'

'No,' said Hope. 'We could start by finding out where that car came from.'

'I'll report it then and we'll see if we can get a hit. I suspect not though. From what I understand, they take these cars in the early hours of the morning. Therefore, everyone's in bed and they've been ditched before anyone gets up.'

'Well, thanks,' said Hope. 'I'll let you get on. Like you say, it's over to me now.'

The man nodded almost in sympathy and shook Hope's hand.

Hope spent the next half an hour surveying the scene and organising colleagues back at the station to start searching through CCTV images on the surrounding area. She got a number plate for the car and the make and set in motion a tracing action to find out where it had been stolen from, but what she really wanted was the second car.

Alan Ross approached her as the dawn was finally coming through, enough to chase the dark away and a red sky was greeting them.

'I found them,' said Alan. 'Managed to round up all the family. Identified the four kids in there. It's pretty much a mess. It seems that the four of them hung around together quite a lot. One of the mums said that they may have broken the rules but they didn't do anything bad. They certainly weren't into drugs, but she isn't surprised that they might have taken a car. They had spoken to them several times about this, each time they promised it wasn't them, but their mothers suspected. I've got a family support officer with them now, so waiting to hear some more information. I haven't told them that we think it's murder yet. I thought we'd save that for the interviews.'

'Good idea,' said Hope, and advised Alan what she'd done in terms of tracing action. From behind her, she heard someone shouting.

'Oi, you, are you in charge?' Hope spun on her heel, glowering over at a woman who seemed to be wrapped up in a coat over the top of a dressing gown.

'Yes,' said Hope. 'Do you have something you need to say?'

'Those wee glyps needed that,' said the woman, almost coldly. 'It's about time someone got their comeuppance raking through here. The wee hours in the morning and they're doing this. Do you know what it's like trying to get a baby to sleep when all you've got is these youths driving back and forward, shouting on the pavements? They don't disappear until the early hours in the morning. Then we have to get up and go to work, but what are they doing? Skipping off school, lying in bed. It's about time something like this happened to them. Don't even know how to drive a car.'

Hope registered that the woman thought this had been an accident, and she certainly wasn't about to dissuade her.

'You tell them, Annie,' said another woman. 'You tell them. That's Gilmartin's kid, isn't it, that's in there? Always getting into fights, pulling stunts, used to nick off the shop on the estate as well, just because he's an Indian gentleman. Think they can just walk in and do what they want instead of trying to make a living like anybody else.'

Hope put her hands up. 'While you're all very entitled to your opinion, can I just make it clear that I'm investigating this? If you wish to make a statement about what's happened, indeed if you saw anything that happened prior to this incident, then please contact my detective constable. He'll gladly take a statement from you.'

Hope glanced at Alan, wondering if he was giving her dagger eyes, but as per usual, Ross had that determined grin on his face; one that said he was professional in all things. Hope watched Ross step forward and begin to talk to the women and calm down what was rapidly becoming a very heated debate. As she watched, from the corner of her eye, she saw a man stumbling forward with a quarter bottle of booze in his hand, supping down hard on it. He was at least six feet four, built like someone born to be a labourer, and from the way his eyes were spinning, it looked like he had consumed much more drink earlier on this evening.

A constable moved to head off the man, advising him that there was an incident, but the man reached out a hand, pushing the constable backwards. The constable took three steps and promptly landed on his backside before he jumped up.

Hope strode across, put a hand up to the constable indicating he should just stand back for a moment, and she looked at the

23

man who had stopped in his tracks on seeing the red haired, six-foot sergeant in front of him. It wasn't always right, but Hope understood that sometimes the use of feminine charm could resolve the situation far quicker than any heavy hand.

'Excuse me. I'm Detective Sergeant Hope McGrath. With an incident going on behind us, you need to stop where you are, sir.'

'They said Johnny's in there.'

'Johnny?' asked Hope. 'Who's Johnny?'

'Johnny's my son,' said the man. 'Let me see my son.' He shoved out with a hand, but Hope stepped to one side, caught the wrist and spun the man's arm up behind his back.

'You take it easy,' said Hope. 'We don't go any closer. You don't want to see what's in there.'

'Don't you tell me what I want to see. I want my Johnny. Is Johnny in there? Let me see if Johnny's in there.'

'Do you have a photograph of Johnny?' asked Hope.

The man reached with his free hand inside his jacket. 'Do you mind letting me loose a minute? I'll see if I can get it.'

He fumbled about, dropping his wallet twice before producing a picture and handing it to Hope. There was a woman, possibly only eighteen or nineteen, holding a baby. 'That's Johnny,' he said. 'That's Johnny.'

'Do you have anything more recent, sir?' asked Hope.

'Only that. I thought I would teach him to drive. I said that, I said, "Don't do it yourself," I said, "I'll teach you to drive." He was going to get a job driving a bus. Good job that, you know?' said the man. 'Is my Johnny inside?'

Hope stood in front of the man. 'I don't know yet, sir. We're still finding out all the details.'

From behind them, there was a cry and a man marched up

towards them. He was shorter than the both of them, but he was spitting feathers.

'Is that you? You dare come round here again?' The tall man turned around. Hope watched the little man march right up to him and shove a finger in his chest.

'You got told to leave Jane alone. I told you. I said ,"You come round here again, I'll do you." Didn't I say that?'

'Johnny is in there,' said the big man, his eyes welling up. 'Johnny's in there.'

'Well, good riddance to him,' said the little guy, causing the big man to begin to rock.

'As for you, you can take this for laying a hand on Jane.'

Hope hadn't clocked the crowbar up the man's back but she did as he swung it towards the man's head. She intervened with a strong hand that pushed the large man onto his backside, the crowbar missing by a few inches. The little man then went to jump on the big man, lifted the crowbar up above his head and Hope snatched it, pulling it violently, almost ripping the man's arms out of their sockets. He gave a loud cry and Hope stripped him of the crowbar, throwing it on the ground before reaching and grabbing a wrist, driving it up behind his back. The constable who had been held in check previously by Hope's hand, ran over and cuffed the little man.

'Take him somewhere else. Find out who he is, why he's doing this, and then take him down to the station. See if he can cool off,' said Hope.

'Will do,' said the constable, and marched the little man out of the area. Hope turned back to the large man who was writhing on the floor.

'Johnny,' he said. 'Johnny.' He rolled over and began to pick the dirt from his clothes. Hope looked around her. *What a mess*, she thought. *What a ruddy mess.*

Chapter 04

Macleod paid a visit to Hope at her crime scene before making his way back to the station. Interviews were being done, CCTV was being checked, and the general running of two murder investigations was well underway. Macleod was content that his team was on top of this, even though it was the early days of the investigation.

No one had witnessed either event, so therefore, they had to drill through who had seen their victims last and where they'd been going, who they'd been talking to, and what trouble there was.

Something bothered Macleod though. In both instances, the weapons used had not been that of the street. Had Peter Olive been knifed to death with a butterfly knife or some sort of similar item, he would have been quite content that they were looking for someone else on the estate. But Peter Olive had been gutted with a weapon more suited to the army. The car also had been taken out with a grenade. It was nearly impossible to get hold of an item such as that in Inverness or maybe it was simply something that had been acquired or found by another person on the estate. But it took quite a bit to operate it in that fashion.

Can you pull up in the car? Can you throw it in through the window and then be out of the way before it exploded?

Macleod prepared himself for a day of reading reports and trying to work out what was going on. He'd left Hope and Clarissa on scene while Ross had returned to the station, briefly organising the interview data and the acquisition of important evidence. It was quite something to have somebody like Ross who could do all this. He made sure all the details were covered, allowing Macleod to sit back and ponder. After all, that's what he got paid for, wasn't it, going through the detail and picking out what was important and what wasn't.

He received a phone call from Jane at approximately midday, and part of him drifted back to the early morning shower. It had only been fifteen minutes, but then again, fifteen minutes was better than nothing. She cheekily told him when he left the force, he could have mornings of this. One part of him felt, 'Why not? Hadn't he done enough already?' He wasn't some sort of reward loyalty card that you added the stickers on and then decided to return.

A part of him still felt he was needed. Hope needed him, still required that refinement before she took over, but he also needed to retire because he was gaining too much notoriety. Too often, he was turning up the crime scenes and he could hear them saying, 'That's Macleod.' The unkind ones instead saying, 'That's the ugly one. Where's the redhead that works with him?' Macleod would saunter past, laughing at the comment.

He stood up from behind his desk to look out into the office. As he approached the door with his coffee cup, he saw Ross already there at the machine.

28

'Fresh batch just going on, sir.'

He'd never been able to stop Ross calling him 'Sir'. To tell you the truth, he had stopped trying. As Macleod handed over his coffee cup, his phone began to ring. He paced back to his desk to answer it. 'Detective Inspector Seoras Macleod.' He stared at the illuminated telephone screen. It was an internal call.

'Sorry, it's Seoras.'

'Seoras, it's upstairs here.'

Upstairs was how the DCI addressed himself, just to make sure that you understood that you were downstairs. Macleod had worked with many DCIs, but this one was beginning to grit on him. If it continued, he may even be forced to retire to get rid of the man.

'Seoras, I've got someone coming up to meet you.'

'Coming up to meet me?'

'Yes, Simon Mackenzie. He's a local councillor. With what's just going on recently on those estates, he wants to come up and have a word. He's got quite a good idea, but I'll let him talk to you about that. Of course, you'll need to say yes to it.'

Macleod shook his head. Chief Inspector Calhoun was proving to be a bigger pain than Macleod ever thought. One of the problems Macleod had was that he didn't call Macleod to give detail about the cases he was working on, but rather, every time he pestered him was to brandish some new idea. Macleod was all for passing information on about a case to a superior, for at the end of the day, that's what it should be about. This man asked Macleod for all sorts of things, things about how to change policing, what a modern Facebook page would look like for the Constabulary. Macleod had absolutely no idea nor any inclination to learn about such things.

'I'm working now. Two cases on the go,' said Macleod.

'Seoras, you know as well as I do that a lot of these things get solved out there with the public.'

This was news to Macleod.

'I think the more people we can get on side, especially local council, the better. I've said that he can come up to meet you now. Just hear what he has to say and then be a good man and agree to it. It'd be good for you anyway. I think you'll enjoy it.'

'I'll enjoy what?' asked Macleod.

'You'll see.' The other end of the phone went dead. Macleod placed his receiver down as well. He looked up out into the outer office and saw a man enter, and Ross intercepting him. He wanted to call Ross, tell him to send the man packing, but he'd be dutiful and hear what the man had to say. Macleod opened his office door and saw Ross directing the man over.

'Detective Inspector, this is Simon Mackenzie. He's a local councillor.'

'I contacted the DCI,' said the man. 'I asked him if I could come up and speak to you.'

'Ah, that one,' said Macleod. 'I'll take you through now. Ross, if you wouldn't mind, bring a couple of coffees in. It'd be much appreciated.'

Ross nodded. As soon as Simon Mackenzie turned his back, he looked at Macleod, raising his eyebrows. Macleod did his best not to roll them, given that the man was standing in front of him.

'If you'd come in, Mr Mackenzie. Take a seat there. Would you like a coffee?'

'I thought you'd basically instructed for one to arrive anyway.'

'Well, I can always drink two,' said Macleod. 'Up to you.'

With a smile, Mackenzie nodded. Ross appeared less than thirty seconds later with two coffees, placing one down in front of the inspector and another in front of Mr Mackenzie.

'I hope you don't mind, Mr Mackenzie, I'm a very busy man. If you could just tell me what this is all about.'

'Well, it's actually about the case that you are now investigating. Thing is, you're the back end of the stick, aren't you? The end of the trail when it comes to these things. We have these estates that are running amok. Things spiral out of control, somebody dies, and then you get called in. Ideally, we don't want you to get called in at all. We want to do a bit of work to make the estate safer and are quite keen for you to get involved.'

Macleod stepped back. Was this a genuine attempt at sorting at the community or was this the constant politician need to be seen to be doing something?

'What are you intending?' asked Macleod.

'For you to go on television; you need to be our lead, promoting it from the front, reaching out to the kids and the youth. You're a well-known figure these days, Inspector.'

'I'm a well-known detective inspector. I hardly think it appropriate for me to sort of dance around.'

'I think you'll find I'm not dancing around, Mr Macleod.'

'I need to run a murder investigation. I'm afraid my time's very limited.'

'Oh, don't worry about that. I've instructed the DCI that I need someone, and he said it's okay for you.'

'No,' said Macleod, 'no way. Why on earth would anybody want me on their TV screen?'

'Hear me out, first of all. Seoras, can I call you Seoras?'

Macleod wanted to say no, absolutely not. The term is detective inspector, and he was not to call him by any other name. Unfortunately, the DCI made it quite clear that Mr Mackenzie was someone to be entertained to some degree, and so Macleod simply nodded reluctantly.

'The thing is you have a certain persona. You seem to be getting results around the city. Everything you seem to step up to ends up sorted. The only one I think got away was that coach bomber.'

Macleod kept a straight face. He knew who had done the coach bombing, a case that had been ended with a man being shot dead in the belief that he was the coach bomber. Macleod knew the woman who had done it and he'd followed her out to another country to tell her so. However, he couldn't prove it and he couldn't bring her back.

'Spoiled goods,' said Macleod. 'No point in having me on. Can probably bring that up every time, like you just have.'

Simon Mackenzie replied, 'Oh, I'm sure we all make mistakes, Inspector.'

That was one, thought Macleod. *That was one.*

'The thing is, you have a unique position. You're old enough that the older generations trust you and yet, you're successful enough and, dare I say it, quirky enough that even the young people seem to dig you.'

Dig me? thought Macleod, a word that never seemed to be used with him and one that he wasn't quite sure he fully understood what it meant. He certainly didn't have a fan club running.

'I want to run a biweekly program that would have you the front cleaning up our estates. I'll come on with you, but we go around the rough areas. You'd be able to talk to people about what the problems are and suggest the way forward. And as things get better, we'd be able to introduce that, show people what was happening, as well as doing some inspiring vignettes.'

'No,' said Macleod very bluntly. 'With all due respect, the reason you're sitting here now is because I was told to entertain you, that you were to come up and say to me what to do with regards to these estates. I have listened and I am saying no. I have two murder cases to get on with, ones that will not solve themselves. I don't have time to be messing about with television.'

'You won't be messing about, Inspector. Trust me. Trust me when I tell you, Seoras, that you are someone who can make a difference.'

In the old days, back in the wild west, Macleod would've been known as someone who could hang them high and, in some ways, he liked to think of himself as that. Someone who came in, solved the problems, caught the bad guys. He did not see himself as a tour guide leading others through that path.

'The answer is still no,' said Macleod. 'Now, I've listened to you, Councillor Mackenzie. I've rejected your idea. Would you kindly let me get on with my investigation now? But do drink your coffee first. Ross made it. It's good.'

Macleod picked up his cup and tried to end the meeting, draining it in one go. 'Like I said, it's good. Well worth taking all in at once.'

'Are you sure I can't change your mind?' said Mackenzie.

'No, you can't.' Macleod advised, 'I don't mean to be rude, but please, can you leave?'

The man stood up, taking a large gulp of his coffee before turning for the door. As he reached it, he turned back.

'The DCI said it should be you with that staff sergeant of yours. McGrath, I think, he called her. Over your shoulder,

33

says you make a good pair. I'm not sure he was talking about the police work.'

'We make a great pair,' said Macleod, 'and it's mainly the police work.'

'So, it's a definite no.'

'It's a definite no,' said Macleod.

'I'll have to speak to the DCI again.'

'You do that, Councillor Mackenzie, but trust me, you won't get any change out of me. I've got a murder to solve.'

Macleod was amazed at how well he kept the secret that the other case was also murder, and he almost beamed as the man left the office.

Ross popped back in inside of an hour and began to give the paperwork to Macleod of the case of the exploded car. Macleod laid it out in the desk in front of him and began reading through, but in his head, he struggled to get rid of the idea of what would happen if the DCI reacted badly to his refusal.

Macleod went through the notes and decided that the investigations would have to stay split for now. He called Hope, advising her that she was to keep the lead in the case of the car while Clarissa would run the other investigation. Macleod would try and sit over the top of both. Once he informed his team what was happening, Macleod sat back down at the desk and began to work. It was about five o'clock when he noticed a figure standing in front of him. She hadn't made a sound as she came through the door, but was now sitting in front of him with a large pizza box.

'How's it going?' Macleod looked up and saw Jane, his partner, staring back at him.

'I don't know about you,' she said, 'but fifteen minutes wasn't

34

really enough.'

Macleod looked around him, and wondered what his woman was wanting here.

'I thought I'd pop in and bring you some dinner. You always manage to forget on the first day. Seems pretty rough what's going on in the estate.

'The estates are nothing,' said Macleod. 'The DCI's trying to make me into a TV star.'

'You don't want it?'

'Well, no. Can you imagine?' said Macleod.

'Still, it's good you're getting noticed.'

'Is it?' queried Macleod. 'Is it, really? The last thing I need is to get noticed,' said Macleod. 'This thing today, it was . . .'

She gave a comforting smile before stopping and looking at Macleod. 'Did you turn them down?'

'Yes,' said Macleod.

'You don't think I could just pop in and take over.'

Macleod shook his head and looked up. He stood up and made his way around the desk to where Jane was sitting. Down on his knees, he put his arms around her. She was something he could count on, always there.

Chapter 05

Ross had gone through all the statements that had been made regarding the joyriders and was still feeling unsatisfied. It seemed to him that there was a certain part of the population that was missing from the statements, mainly the friends of those who had died. Ross looked up the names of those who had died and wondered if he should approach the school? Or were any of them in school? He thought about going to clubs, youth groups, but again, he wondered if they were even there.

Ross had no kids of his own. He felt he missed out on understanding what kids or teenagers did. Instead, he started to walk around the estate, to see if he could find any of them. Would the friends just be kicking about? After all, that's what people did at the time of bereavement. They came together, came together to talk about the person, share their feelings. Surely, they'd be missing their friends. Surely, there'd be something within them that would require them to share what was normal. That's what humans did. They got themselves together to talk through their grief.

Rather than take the car out, Ross strolled around the estate, passing by the local playpark, then by a shop front where he saw a number of youths. They seemed younger than the victims within the cars. He continued to walk on. It was at the end of the street beneath a large streetlight, which seemed to be on despite the fact that it was the middle of the day, that Ross found a large group congregating, some twelve youths. He pitched them at anything from fourteen to seventeen, but given his track record for guessing ages at a time of life when people grew at such a varied fashion that their size and shape didn't seem to fit the norm, he recognised that he may be wrong.

'Do you mind if I have a word with you?' asked Ross.

The youth looked up at him, one of them snarling, 'What do you want?'

'I want to talk about Johnny and his friends in the car. I'm Detective Constable Alan Ross.' Ross held up his credentials, but none of the youths really looked.

'What happened to them? Some people are saying it wasn't an accident; some people are saying that somebody killed them.'

'Who's saying that?' asked Ross.

'The oldies. People are saying that there was a grenade found in the car.'

It was bound to get out, thought Ross. You couldn't keep these things in, after all. It was Macleod's murder team that were on the case. If it had been Traffic branch in charge, people would have taken it as a simple accident.

'We are investigating whether or not they were murdered,' said Ross.

'Murdered? You mean somebody did kill them; somebody did throw a grenade in?'

'That's correct,' said Ross. He felt very out of place dressed in his shirt and tie and what was a reasonably practical and smart suit. The kids opposite wore a mix of T-shirts and jackets, and where Ross really stood out was this beaming polite face instead of the scowl that teenage angst produced.

'Any of you seen a grenade before?' asked Ross.

'You think we did it?'

'No,' said Ross. 'You're the friends, aren't you? I wanted to know if you'd seen one about the estate. Grenades don't grow on trees.'

'Neither do coppers around here,' said one small lad.

'You don't think there's enough of them?' asked Ross.

'Well, clearly there wasn't, was there? Somebody walked in with a grenade and killed Johnny and the rest of them.'

'Well, I'm here to try and find out who did it.' Ross watched one of the kids in the back take out a bottle of what he presumed was vodka and start to drink it. His first instinct looking at the young man was to ask him his age, but there were more important things happening at the moment and he needed what they knew rather than give them a load of aggro for underage drinking.

'You want some, copper?'

'No,' said Ross, 'and if I did drink vodka, I wouldn't be drinking that. Have you seen where they make it?' The kid looked at the bottle and looked at Ross, and then shrugged his shoulders before dropping down another slug.

'Does anyone in this estate have access to those kinds of weapons?' asked Ross.

'Why our estate?' said one of the lads. 'Why would we or anybody here want to do that? Johnny was a hero; he nicked all the best cars. You see, he was a legend, always did the best cars.'

'Where did he go to get them?' asked Ross, already knowing that the car had been traced to a city centre apartment.

'Bus into town, car back,' said the guy. 'That was the thing. Johnny would actually go into town, drink a bit, and then go nick something for the trip back, but he was impressing women. He liked to impress the girls that way.'

'Are you girls impressed with that?' asked Ross, quite flatly.

'Nothing else around here, is there? Nothing else to do except the best sex and a bit of fun.'

'She knows all about sex,' said another. A small fistfight broke out, which Ross did nothing to stop, instead simply standing and waiting for it to calm down again.

'The man who he stole the car off lives in one of the big apartments blocks in the centre of town,' said Ross. 'He must have done well to nick it.'

'You think? Older cars, the older ones are the best ones to nick because they don't have the same locks and they don't have the same codes to get past; you don't need the keys.'

'Did he do any drugs, do you know?'

There was a bit of laughter.

'What did I say?' asked Ross. 'I'm quite straight about this. Did he do any drugs?'

'No,' said one of the other guys. 'He didn't move them about, didn't sell them on, and he didn't take himself. He might have got the very odd pill, but that was about it. When he went out for a night, a little bit of something, not much, not serious gear. He wasn't a junkie; neither was he somebody who would move it on for them either.'

'You think somebody put a grenade in because he was doing drugs? You think somebody actually thought he was a drug dealer?' asked a different boy.

'I don't know what to think,' said Ross. 'That's why I'm asking. I don't live here, not from here, so I need to work out why somebody would throw a grenade in their car.'

Ross sat down on top of a nearby wall and was suddenly flanked by two of the older guys.

'Did you say your name was Ross?'

'That's right,' said Ross, suddenly feeling that there was a hike in the tension.

'You work for Macleod, don't you?'

'That's correct,' said Ross. 'You got a problem with him?'

'No. You're the gay cop, aren't you? You're bent.'

Ross was, in some ways, slightly taken aback. He was used to the idea that people didn't like his sexuality, but generally it came from older people. The younger crowd pretty much seemed to accept the way people were these days. In fact, many were quite the advocates for it. Ross never brought his sexuality into work. Generally, he kept quiet about it unless asked. He never saw the point in provoking the bear. In this case, the bear had come looking for him.

'I'm a homosexual,' he said, 'that's correct. You got a problem with that?'

'Your sort are all the same, aren't they? Aren't you? Do you think he really is,' asked the girl in the crowd, 'or does he just do it because it looks cool?'

'Oh, shut up, Janine,' said another voice. 'Of course, he is. He barely even looks at you. Look, he's not even looking at me.' Ross caught from the corner of his eye the girl pull her top up and flash him before quickly putting it back down again.

'You're not even embarrassed or excited about that, are you? Total bender.'

'I think it's more important that we talk about your friends

40

and about who killed them,' said Ross. 'You might not like who I have in my life. Now, that's up to you,' he said. 'Frankly, I don't care, but I do care who killed your friends.'

'Bloody big poof,' said the boy beside him, and Ross felt a smack across the back of his head. He'd hit him hard. He bent over and doubled, putting his hand up and feeling the back of his head. When he brought his hand right in front of him, there was blood.

'Right,' he said, and turned to the guy but felt someone kick him at the back of the ankles. A punch went into his kidneys.

'What are you doing?' said a voice, and Ross recognised Hope. Her Glaswegian brogue was evident anywhere and she was using it to full effect now. 'Get your hands off him now, or I'll haul the lot of you down to the station.'

'What are you doing working with a poof like this?' one of the guys said. Hope grabbed him, turned him around and handcuffed him. 'That is a hate crime for which I'll take you down the station and book you and we'll sit and have a chat and we'll keep you in there as long as I possibly can before I actually make sure that you get fined properly.' Hope glanced over at Ross and saw his bloodied hand.

'Which one of you hit him?' There wasn't a sound, but Ross stood up, grabbed the wrist of one of the boys, twisted it and a knuckle duster fell off his hand.

'Ah. Bloody hell, copper. You can't do that to me. That's harassment. That's bullying.'

'That's arresting someone who's just assaulted him,' said Hope. 'You've assaulted him for being gay. That's a hate crime and currently they'll throw the book at you for that.'

Ross walked back to the wall and sat down, took a handkerchief out from his pocket, placed it on the back of his head.

'You don't want to be fighting us,' he said. 'You need to understand. Somebody came around here, put a grenade in the car of your friends. If you go joyriding, if you go and do something else, what's to stop them putting a grenade in with you? Who's doing this? Who has a grudge against your friends so big that they'd actually throw a grenade in a car?

'It's like a wall of silence here. There's a load of people telling me that Johnny was trouble, that his friends were trouble, that you wreck this estate. Half of this estate would be quite happy to see you lot end up the same way. That's what's being said when I interview people. Frankly, if we were to arrest you now and take you downtown, this whole estate would cheer us on. I don't think anyone in this estate is going to wing a grenade into a car. Who do you provoke that badly?'

'Warmsley, they don't like us,' said one young lad. 'They're always over here trying to get at us, trying to show off if they can get the better cars, trying to show off with their gear.'

'Warmsley estate,' said Hope, 'the gangs over there?'

'Yes, they ain't much,' said one of them. 'They ain't anything; we're miles better than them. Much tougher.'

'So tough you just got handcuffed by a female copper,' said Hope. She was aware of one of the young lads looking up at her.

'You are fine, aren't you?' he said. 'Stacked as well.'

Hope had to bite her tongue because she wanted to go over and smack the guy around the head, tell him off for being so cheeky, but part of her was quite impressed with the words. They were vulgar, but yes, she looked good. She clocked a few of the other boys who were looking, but the girls seemed quite put out by her.

'I don't need any more comments about how I look. I don't

need any more comments about the sexuality of my friend. What I need to know is if Johnny or any of his cohorts managed to cheese off the Warmsley gang.'

'Three months ago, he was over that way. He picked up one of their girls, did the business and that. Apparently, it was one of their guy's birds. They weren't too happy about it.'

'Three months ago,' said Ross. 'They still holding that grudge?'

'If somebody did your bird, how would you feel? Oh yes, that's right, you don't have one.' There was a smattering of laughter which quickly dried up when Hope stared around at them.

'I said, is there any other reason? That's not a bad one. Anything else though?'

'They don't need a reason, do they? It's Warmsley. We're not that far from each other. They know as they isn't the best, they know we're tougher, they knows what we can do.'

'Do you always congregate here?' asked Hope.

'Under the light, because it's always on, you see.'

'How did that happen?' asked Ross.

'It's not difficult. We're not dumb. We can do some electrics and that.' Hope looked over at Ross's hand again. When he'd taken it off his head, the white handkerchief was stained red with blood.

'Just let me tell you,' said Hope. 'You give my constable anymore grief or I get another comment about my body from any of you, I will haul you downtown shoved into handcuffs. Until then, don't do anything daft. I would stay off the street at night and I wouldn't nick any cars. If somebody's throwing grenades about, you don't want to be in the line of fire.' Again, there was a bit of laughter. 'I mean it,' said Hope. 'Over in

43

Warmsley, somebody knifed someone to death with a proper knife and did it time and time again, left them lying in a pool of blood. Stay off the streets after dark until we wrap this up.'

Hope went over to help Ross, but he waved her away, standing up and walking ahead of her. As she departed, she heard the wolf whistles behind her and a cry of, 'That arse.' She wondered what John, her partner would say. Would he laugh? She certainly hoped he would agree. Then she had a feeling. These boys, she could see where the people on the estate got off wanting them dead, wanting them out of the way, because at the moment she was struggling to see why they were like the way they were and why they couldn't change.

Chapter 06

Clarissa had the same idea as Ross and had taken to the street, looking for any of the kids that had been hanging around at the time Peter Olive had died. The hours previous were important to Clarissa, and so far, the interviews around the estate had yielded nothing. People didn't want to talk too much. Even the adults, those who were against the youths who were causing trouble, said very little. Sure, they would berate how they ran about here and there, but when you got to the specifics of who saw what and when, everyone said very little. There was a definite culture of fear on the estate.

It was one, in fairness, uniform had warned her about. They tried to get a hold of the estate and had launched various schemes and initiatives. Things had seemed to be spiralling, getting worse. Despite this, Clarissa needed answers, although she was aware she was operating in a very foreign environment. When you worked for the art division looking into thefts of an expensive nature and amongst a higher class of society, you had to fit into various conventions. You appeared looking the part, you had to know your art, and you had to be able to smell a forgery a mile away.

Clarissa thought anyone watching her walk this street would be smelling a forgery. She wasn't the estate cop, wasn't someone who knew how these places operated, but she was Macleod's Rottweiler. It wasn't a name that she normally appreciated, but it was one she was reciting to herself, and she walked along the now dark street.

Clarissa came upon the play park in the middle of the Warmsley estate and could see several youths, probably towards the end of their teens. They were milling about, quiet, eyes peering out towards her. There was little joy and laughter, but she did notice a few bottles sitting around. Clarissa lifted her shoulders, decided she needed to talk to these people because they looked like Peter Olive's age and they were dressed similarly to him. She was aware, however, in her tartan trousers and boots and with a shawl flung around her shoulders that she certainly didn't look the part for them.

'What's up with you, grandma?' someone shouted as Clarissa wandered over. She kept her head lifted, staring at the boy who had said it, eyes piercing him.

'Did you guys know Peter Olive?'

'What the hell's it to you?' Clarissa looked down at where the voice had come from. That kid was only about fourteen. Why'd she then get off speaking to Clarissa like that?

'I'm Detective Sergeant Clarissa Urquhart and I need to find who killed Peter. I need to talk to you boys. Oh, and girls.' Clarissa almost added a grunt of disapproval. When she saw the girl at the back, she thought there was enough earrings on her to make her ears permanently droop for life, and as for the ring through the nose, Clarissa never understood why anybody wanted to look like a bull. *And they think what I wear is garish.*

'Well, we don't want to talk to you, do we?' said one boy.

'That's all right,' said Clarissa. 'You're entitled not to speak, but you'll be entitled not to speak down at the station. I have inquiries to carry out. If you're going to refuse to answer any questions, we're going to make sure that's recorded formally.'

'Get out of it, grandma. Can't you see we're busy here?'

'You don't look busy to me. You look like you're having some alcohol you shouldn't, and let's be honest, most of you can't hold that. You're milling about doing nothing.'

'There's nothing to do.'

'Bollocks.' Clarissa saw the shocked looks on their faces and they didn't expect it of her with the shawl and the trousers, thinking she was upper class. It was funny how they all thought that people of her ilk spoke properly when in fact, they could swear and curse with the best of them.

'Yes, you heard me,' said Clarissa. 'We'll drag you down one by one and we'll sit you down one by one, away from your friends and I'll ask questions.'

'You can't do that. We're not eighteen.'

'That's true. We'll have somebody else in with you, either your parent or we'll have one of those social workers who's probably getting to the end of their day and thinking, I can't be bothered with these people anymore. They'll just sit there while we continue. Oh, we can't do it for that long, but we still have the questions to ask. Obviously, we'll have to keep you for a lot longer. More than that; if you're not answering any questions about Peter, we're clearly going to think you've got something against him.'

'What do you mean?' asked one of the boys.

'Somebody took a knife and drove it into the gut of your supposed friend, Peter Olive. How am I meant to know why

47

they did that? I mean, did he fancy you, love?'

The girl looked sheepish, and Clarissa thought maybe she'd hit something on the head. 'Or maybe he'd gone for somebody else. Maybe you couldn't handle that. Maybe you fancy her as well,' said Clarissa, pointing at another boy. 'This isn't play time. Somebody hasn't put a brick through the head teacher's window at the school. Somebody drove a knife into the gut of Peter Olive and they did it again and again and again, and they made sure that he bled out, that he died in pain. Now, there's two things about that,' said Clarissa, 'but you won't be quick enough to work them all out.'

'Well, you reckon one of us might have done it,' said the lad who had spoken first. 'You reckon it's one of us so you want to know reasons why.'

'That's one way to look at it,' said Clarissa, 'but there is another.'

She looked at blank faces, and she began to understand why. There was almost an invincibility when they stood together in a crowd. That's why they weren't seeing it.

'Peter Olive was here with you. From what I can gather, this is where he hung out. I'm suspecting he was here the night he died, or rather this morning when he died.'

'Well, yes,' said one boy. 'He was here with us.'

'The killer went after him. What if it's not Peter Olive they were after?'

One of the other boys looked up. 'What do you mean? Of course, it was him they were after. They killed him and you said they were up close and cutting him, drove the knife in several times. Why would they do that if they didn't think it was him?'

'What I'm saying is,' and Carissa stepped forward putting a

48

foot up onto a short, small wall and leaning both her forearms on her knee, coming down almost to their level, 'what if it wasn't Peter specifically, they were after? What if they just wanted one of you?'

There were a few agitated looking faces until somebody blurted out. 'Why would they want us?'

'Noise through the night intimidating the younger kids. I mean, I've heard it all. There's some joy riding goes on around the place, drug scene on street corners. I mean, quite frankly, you're turning this, what should be a reasonably good estate, into a crappy one, aren't you?'

'You don't get to talk to me like that,' said one boy stepping forward. He was six foot tall, far taller than Clarissa, but she never flinched, keeping both her forearms on top of her knee. Inside, she started to feel a little bit panicked. Maybe she should have brought someone with her. That was the thing about art thieves. They were much more subtle. They didn't come back in your face quite like this.

'I don't have to say any of it. All the people right here are saying it. Adults, people with young kids. You do realise that they'll dump you lot in it. I wouldn't be surprised if some people are half happy that Peter Olive is dead.'

'Peter was part of our gang,' said a younger kid. A hand went out from one of the older boys telling him to shut up.

'Gang, is it?' said Clarissa. 'Maybe this is a gang thing then. Who's the gang rival then? Who's the one you all don't like? Come on. There's got to be one. You don't have gangs on their own. Gangs are always formed in pairs at least, if not more. Who is it you don't like?'

'Knockmalley,' said one kid, stepping forward. 'I've knocked the hell out of them.'

'Shush,' said one of the guys at the front. 'We don't talk to cops. You don't talk to the police.'

'Someone's dead,' said Clarissa. 'You can play your games all you want, but until we find out who's killed him, they could come back for you.'

'We don't talk to your type,' said one boy.

Clarissa nodded and started to walk off until she saw the girl doubling up in pain.

'What's up with you, love?' asked Clarissa.

'We told you, we don't talk to you.'

'Shut up,' said Clarissa, turning to the guy. 'It's a woman's thing. You might not understand. Cramps, is it, love? Come with me. See what we can do for you.' The girl with the earrings that seemed infeasibly numerous for the size of her ears limped over towards Clarissa who identified it immediately as having nothing to do with period cramps. She put an arm around the girl, helped her around the corner, and noticed some of the boys starting to follow.

'Just get back. This is women's things,' said Clarissa. 'You know, sometimes women need each other. Go on. Just go.'

She could see that most of the boys were uncomfortable with what she'd said and turned away almost instantly, but the one who had spoken first was watching her carefully. Clarissa stood her ground until he disappeared back around the corner.

Clarissa put her hand down just below the girl's belly and whispered in her ear. 'There's nothing wrong with you at all. In all my years, I've never seen somebody bend like that, not that they'll know. What's up?'

'Peter Olive was talking to Jake Hughes the night he died. He threatened him. That's all I know. I was here and I heard it. It's not good, is it?'

'Were you fond of Peter?' asked Clarissa.

'Yes, I was, but it's not good.' The girl stood up and went to walk around the corner and Clarissa grabbed her shoulder. 'Don't walk round there like nothing's wrong. I suggest you put your hand over where they think it would be sore. Give it a few minutes and then you go home. At least it'll look reasonable to them because that guy who spoke first, he doesn't believe you now. You go back around looking perfect and he's going to ask questions.'

Clarissa wasn't expecting a thanks, but it was almost an imperceptible nod the girl gave. At least her hand went down to below her belly, and she limped back round the corner.

Clarissa walked back to the mobile unit and looked up some information for Jake Hughes. Finding the address, she strode out to the semi-detached house. It looked reasonably new, and outside was one of those air source heat pumps, the new-fangled kind that hadn't been installed twenty years ago. With a knock on the door, she found a woman in a dressing gown who looked blurry-eyed at her.

'Detective Sergeant Clarissa Urquhart. I need to speak to Jake Hughes. Are you his mum?'

'Yes. It's just me and Jakey in here. I've been trying to get him to sleep, but he's not going to sleep.'

'I think I know why,' said Clarissa. 'May I come in?'

The woman showed Clarissa along the hallway to a small bedroom where a youth of maybe thirteen was sitting under his covers, his head barely poking out. The boy's face was white almost as if in terror.

'Jake, my name is Clarissa. I'm with the police.' The boy stuck his head under the covers.

'I'm not talking to you.'

51

'Why is that?' asked Clarissa.

Behind her, she heard the mum say, 'Jake, you need to talk to them. Tell them what's wrong.'

'What's wrong is that Peter Olive talked to Jake not long before he died. He threatened Jake. Didn't he?' The covers moved back. The pair of eyes looked out. 'Look, Jake, I'm not coming for you,' said Clarissa. 'I just wanted to know. Did you see anyone else?'

'I didn't do anything. I didn't go after him,' said the boy. 'I wasn't anywhere near him. When they left, I got away. I came back here. It's just some people say I did it.'

Clarissa looked at the youth in front of her and thought about the number of times Peter Olive had been stabbed. It was also with a knife that would look large and unwieldy in this boy's hands.

'I don't think you did it. I don't think you're strong enough to do it, nor do you have the height.' In an earlier briefing, forensics had spoken about how the knife was driven in. This kid would've had to push it up. It would've lost all force. He was too small for the height of Peter Olive. 'What I need to know is,' said Clarissa, 'did he say anything? Did you overhear anything about somebody else not liking Peter? Having a problem?'

'No,' said Jake. 'We just keep to ourselves and then they come along to the playground, and they throw us off. They shout at us. You see what they're drinking and the drugs they're taking sometimes. I'm not allowed that.'

'Good,' said Clarissa. 'I'm going to get to the bottom of this. Don't worry.' Clarissa turned to the mother, indicating that she go back out into the hallway.

'You might want to keep an eye on him over the next couple

of days. Kids do stupid things when rumours get out. We'll get to the bottom of this but until then, I'd keep a special eye on it, on anybody who'd think he'd do anything like that. It's crazy. He's not got the strength to do it.'

'He's not like that,' said his mum.

'Maybe not,' said Clarissa, 'I wouldn't know; I don't know him. What I'm saying is, I don't think he could have done it, but out there, they won't accept that until we find somebody else, so keep him safe.' The woman thanked Clarissa and showed her to the door. As it shut behind her, Clarissa wondered how else to get in amongst the teens to find out about Peter Olive's enemies. Everything was so close-knit.

She was walking back towards where the mobile unit was and found a street where the lights had gone out. As she walked along in the dark, Clarissa had a sudden feeling. She looked around but there was no one there. She continued to walk, hearing the heels of her boots clipping the paving stones, and then she heard another sound as well. It was like the rub of a sneaker, a little squeak, as if it had been placed on the wrong surface, or had somebody stumbled. She turned around again, but there was no one there. When she turned back, Clarissa suddenly found a hand on her throat, and she was pushed back up against the wall.

She was looking into the face of the youth who had spoken first. He was taller than her, approaching six feet. His arms were strong. She thought he must be approaching maturity, possibly seventeen or eighteen. One hand held a knife. It wasn't big or sophisticated, one of the simple butterfly ones that you could tuck well away but it had a sharp edge on it.

'You need to sort this, grandma. You hear me? Don't come around and threaten us. We didn't do it. None of us did it.'

53

'Then you need to tell me who did; you need to tell me.'

'We don't need to tell you nothing; you just need to solve it. Go out and find who did this, then tell me and I'll go get them.'

'That's not how it works,' said Clarissa, and felt the hand on her throat closing tightly, so much so that she began to choke.

'I didn't ask you what you wanted to do, I told you what I wanted.'

Did this guy really think he could threaten her, and then she'd come back and give him all this information? Didn't he realise she had an entire police force on her side that'd just go and pick him up for threatening an officer?

'Maybe I'll leave you a little mark just so you understand the terms of our deal.'

The youth put the knife towards Clarissa's face, looking to move in on her cheek. She tried to breathe deeply, but the hand on her throat was strong. Yet the boy wasn't sensible. He left both of Clarissa's hands free, obviously believing that a hand on her throat was going to hold her. She swung the first hand in on his throat, causing him to choke while her other arm came forward and put two fingers straight into his eyes. As he stumbled backwards, she kicked him hard, and he fell to the ground. She strode quickly over, stomping a foot on his wrist, making sure the knife dropped before kicking it clear. She knelt, her knee going straight into his stomach.

'Let's get something straight here, Junior. I'm going to go and find this killer and I will arrest them, and I'll put them in jail and make sure they're locked up for a long time. You, however, will not come near me or threaten me again because if you do, I'll put my warrant card down and I'll put you through that wall, sunshine, and I'll leave you in a state where you can't threaten any grandmas again. Are we clear?'

The boy went to answer, but Clarissa pushed down with her knee on his stomach and he struggled to get the words out. 'We're clear,' he said eventually, as Clarissa stood up looking at him as he tried to crawl up onto his knees first and start getting some large lungsful of air. Having done so, he went over for his butterfly knife, but she told him to leave it. He turned and looked at her before spitting, 'You're a psycho,' and he ran off.

Clarissa could feel the sweat underneath her shawl because he really had throttled her good. Maybe next time she'd come with an escort. She looked at her left hand and saw it was shaking slightly. *Not bad for my age*, she thought, but if there had been a group of them . . . With that undesirable contemplation on her mind, she strode off, back to the mobile unit and the comfort of police numbers.

Chapter 07

J ona Nakamura had given the final forensic report on the two murder scenes, none of which elicited anything of great use to Macleod. The car did have a grenade thrown into it, and now Jona was trying to get the pieces back together to see if she could identify it correctly, and then hopefully chase down where it came from. They said it would take time.

The car had been taken into the compound to be worked upon, and Macleod knew it wouldn't be anytime soon before he got an answer. The murder weapon for the death of Peter Olive had not been found either, but Jona had stated that it would have been wielded by someone who could use it with force. The size of the blade meant it was unlikely that anyone of moderate strength had used it and the cut, each one had been forceful, driven in either with passion or more likely, said Jona, with technique.

With the number of stab wounds, she thought that Peter Olive would have died quicker, but all the organs like the heart, the ones that would have meant he would have been put out of his misery quicker, had been avoided. Instead, whoever had killed Peter Olive knew where to put a knife to cause him agony and pain and to bleed out.

They'd also been clever enough to sneak off to a spot without a CCTV camera to commit the murder, but also not to be seen arriving on the estate. Ross and other members of the team had been through the CCTV of the area, and they had struggled to find anything untoward. Wherever the killer had parked up, if indeed they had, or wherever they had come from, they had done it in simple fashion.

The car that had pulled up alongside had a tyre tread that was extremely standard. It was available at many of the local tyre companies. Until they could find other cars with other connections to the murder, it wasn't going to be useful. However, once they knew what the other car was, it could confirm it was at the scene.

Of course, if the killer was thorough, those tyres would be burning somewhere, and a new set being fitted. Ross had already reached out to many garages, but given the number of cars that were having tyres changed, it was a fruitless task. He could cross-reference with the CCTV of the area but really, it was quite ridiculous.

Besides, if someone was that thorough, they'd have bought the tyres separately, possibly even several months before, and disposed of them after the crime. There were always ways around these things. That didn't stop Macleod putting Ross on it and asking him to go through the paperwork and images.

Clarissa had also reported her little incident to Macleod on the quiet, deciding not to put it into writing. This annoyed Macleod. These days, she seemed to be quite happy to talk about any indiscretions she had. There'd been better ways to handle those kids, but Clarissa being Clarissa had just gone in bull-nosed. Still, it wasn't going to come back and bite them, and she had put the fear of God into them.

Hope was also struggling to make connections in the community, and every report he had was so general. These kids cause trouble, these kids do this, the kids do that, and yet nobody would give specific times and dates. There was a culture of fear about them. Macleod wondered if this is because they'd been let loose for too long.

When he'd grown up, if you stepped out that much, somebody would have put you back in your place. These days, you couldn't even tell them off. People wondered where the right of self-defence even began. The way they spoke to their elders. They also drank openly on the street, something that in Macleod's day would have been frowned upon and dealt with.

Macleod had completed all the courses on social justice, social injustices, why things happened, how estates had gone into these situations. Generally, in his life, he just left it alone because he didn't live on one, he wasn't there, he didn't have to work amongst it. Now a murder was being brought onto his doorstep, and he'd have to understand the climate of what was going on. Still, his gut said that it wasn't an estate problem—it was something else. A grenade and a knife—a serrated knife—and the method of dispatch, not hitting the known vital organs, and making the victim suffer. Macleod was looking for somebody that currently was not in the picture.

Five minutes later, Macleod was summoned into a call with the Chief Constable, something that he didn't have the pleasure of too often. The call was done on his laptop, and thankfully, he managed to navigate his way onto the call, despite the fact Ross wasn't in the office. Also in the call was the Detective Chief Inspector, his boss, and Macleod was worried a setup was in progress. However, the Chief Constable was a woman who didn't take a lot of nonsense, someone who was practical as Macleod saw it, even if she was a little bit more flirtatious with the media than he would have liked.

The discussion centred around the estates of Warmsley and Knockmalley in Inverness and how they were spiralling out of control. Macleod was there to offer updates on how the murder investigation was continuing, but in truth, the real problem was that after a first night of calm, the youth had started to get worried and begun to cause real trouble.

The rumour going around was that this was gang-related, one had killed the other, something that Macleod wasn't buying for an instant. That, however, didn't matter because the youth of the area were out in force; some were marching for peace, as they put it. Decent kids, probably, Macleod had thought, while others were out throwing stones, bricks, and the uniform presence on the estates had been escalated.

Two days on from the murder had seen a number of flashpoint incidents, but now passing tea time and with dark coming soon, the Chief Constable was worried about what might happen this evening. Police officers had been drafted in from many areas to try and control the estates, but there was a serious worry that something untoward was going to happen.

'We need this solved soon, Seoras,' said the Chief Constable.

'I'm on it, Janice. I really am. We've got a problem though in that the culture of the area means they don't speak, they don't talk. Whoever killed Peter Olive and whoever put our four joyriders alight, again, they're good, avoided the CCTV, very difficult to link in. We're waiting for Jona to come up with something, but that's unlikely and, frankly, a shot in the dark. Normally during murders, we can go into the background, find the connections, but I'm not buying the idea of a simple gang warfare. I can't find an initiating action. Why has this changed?

'Over the last six months, the estates haven't been good. You get lots of joyriding. You get people angry with each other,' said Macleod. 'You get the odd street fight. Even the odd gang confrontation. A few stones being thrown, the odd fight, somebody has a broken leg afterwards, but it's not like this. This is a step up and it's too well managed.'

'Who are you thinking?' asked the Chief Constable.

'If I may cut in,' said the Detective Chief Inspector, Macleod's boss, causing Macleod to almost roll his eyes, 'we may be looking for a better trained young person. A young person maybe who has seen some action elsewhere. Maybe newcomer to the area taking over one of the gangs.'

'With all due respect,' said Macleod, 'there's no evidence for that. There's no indication that anyone else has come in and whipped up these gangs. I have a feeling this is an outside influence.'

'I've learned to listen to that feeling over the years,' said the Chief Constable. 'Seoras, we need this nipped in the bud quick, because these estates are starting to erupt. I've had officers attacked today. We've been out in riot uniform. We haven't done that for years. We certainly haven't done it anywhere up near Inverness. Get me the killers. Get me them quick.'

After coming off the call, Macleod had sat, coffee in hand, going over the evidence in his head, wondering if he missed anything. It wasn't like the Chief Constable to speak like this. She was more au fait with the issues that these estates suffered from. If she was calling it going out of control, it quite probably was going to go that way. He pulled over the files again and started looking through them. There'd be something there, something he missed.

* * *

Jai Smith picked up the bottle and threw it hard. He watched it smash on the riot shield of a police constable and laughed, turning around to pick up another one, throwing it again. Beyond him, he saw Daz lighting the top of a Molotov cocktail. Jai raced over to pick it up.

'That's mine, you little bugger,' said Daz. 'Jai, I already had it lit. I'm just throwing it.'

Jai watched it land, the fire licking along the street, a beacon in the night. He didn't even have a mask on and was having the time of his life. Sure, things had kicked off badly, Peter Olive being dead. It was wrong and somebody was going to pay for it. He didn't know who, but he would make sure that somebody did something about it.

Jai heard the charge of the police and turned and ran down the road as they stormed along after him. There were plenty of youths running around, and as they broke, Jai knew he had to get away, go and hide somewhere so the cops couldn't get him. He watched plenty turned right, heading back into the centre of the estate, but he cut off down a separate path at the back of an old abandoned house, holding himself up against the wall and breathing heavily. He heard the cops run by in the street outside and he started to almost laugh.

Not yet, he thought. *Not yet. They're not away yet.* It took a couple of minutes before the noise had moved off to a different part of the estate. The running battles were still in progress, but Jai was out of the way. He crouched down, breathing in huge draughts, half exhausted from his exertions. He remembered how that bottle had broken, the line of fire spreading out from it. That policewoman, she jumped. She totally jumped.

There was a noise coming from the end of the house that he was holed up against. It was like a can had been knocked over.

'Who's there?' shouted Jai. 'Did you get away too?'

There came no answer, but Jai could see a pair of combat trousers. They were grey and black and he thought they were cool, street camouflage. *Neat*, he thought. Next he saw a buckle and a knife in its sheath hanging off a belt.

'Guess we shouldn't talk too loudly,' he said to whoever it was. 'What are you doing here? I had to nip out. They charged and I think they've gone onto the middle of the estate. Do you want to follow them? See what else we can . . .'

A hand reached down and grabbed Jai's hand, pushing it up against the wall in an action that was too quick for him to almost comprehend. He saw a drill bit going into his wrist, just below his hand. He went to scream, but a hand went over his mouth and a knee came up, pushing his body against the wall. Jai watched in horror as he realised it wasn't a drill bit but a masonry screw that was being pushed into the wall through his wrist. His muffled cries went nowhere as he was suddenly kneed in the gut before his other wrist was taken and put up against the wall to have a screw nail pushed through it.

He tried to yell, but a direct blow to his throat took the wind out of him and he couldn't say anything. By the time he'd started to recover, he found himself gagged, barely able to issue a cry at all. The figure opposite him was dressed in full street combat gear with a black balaclava on as well. He could see eyes looking at him with hate, but the figure said nothing.

Instead, it produced several bottles and Jai cried as the first was picked up and thrown hard at him. It cracked off his skull, landed on the ground, but didn't break. Jai's head rang, a bruise quickly forming on his forehead. He shook off the blow, looking at the figure in front of him, not comprehending why this was happening.

The figure almost looked disgusted, took the bottle that was on the ground, cracked it off the wall, causing it to break, leaving lots of jagged edges, and then took another couple and started breaking them too. Jai watched in horror as it then picked these bottles up and threw them at Jai.

The next three minutes were the most painful of Jai's life. At times, he thought he would black out, wished he would go, just disappear into an oblivion without pain, but instead he found himself abused with these broken bottles, unable to get off the wall, his arms firmly screwed to it. He was then doused with what he thought was paraffin or at least something like that. He watched the figure in front of him take a Molotov cocktail and light the rag that was in it. Those eyes again, full of hate and anger. The last image he saw was the bottle being thrown towards him.

Chapter 08

'I'm taking you down.'

'I don't need a babysitter.'

'Seoras, this is serious. These places are alive at the moment. We need to close ranks, stay tight together.'

'Jona is down there,' said Macleod. 'It can't be that bad.'

'Jona is down there inside a ring of protection where riot police cordoned off the entire area. We've got more of them running around, trying to get the area back under control. This murder's just made it even worse. I am driving you down.'

Macleod had never seen Hope so vehement in what she was saying. He knew why she was like this, wanting to protect him, but sometimes he felt like a fuddy-duddy.

'Seoras, she's right. When I got attacked, I was lucky they didn't come in a group. The way things are now, somebody will do something stupid. We need to be not on the receiving end of that.'

Clarissa and Hope, in agreement, looked over at Ross.

'We all go in together, sir,' said Ross. 'The sergeants are correct. We all go together. We move in and out as a team.'

Macleod grabbed his coat and quickly strolled down to the car park where there was a large police van that he hadn't seen in a while. Across the windscreen was a large grill. Each of the windows were the same.

'These guys are part of the team looking after the estate,' said Hope. 'They'll get us in, and they'll get us back out again. We don't muck about.'

Macleod acquiesced and sat at the rear of the van, allowing himself to be driven in. As they got closer to the estate, he could see the fires burning, cars alight, and yet they seemed to be taken away from what had been the main centre of rioting. They arrived at the police cordon that moved to one side, letting them in.

Macleod stepped out of the van. Everywhere was the smell of smoke and burning. Macleod tasted it in his mouth and nose. He could feel the tension in the air. *I wondered how it was for the residents of the estate. Hopefully barricading in their homes.* A sudden thought came to him.

'Jake Hughes, you went and saw him, Clarissa. Is he . . .'

'We moved him and his mum out. They're in a hotel somewhere, well clear. We're keeping an eye on the house, and we made sure everybody knew they weren't in the house. I think it's not really about them. It's not a case of rioting, it's just a case of just turning everything upside down.'

Macleod nodded. He was about to walk over to what he presumed was the crime scene at the side of one of the houses, when he saw the Chief Constable's assistant, who had come up to Inverness. The man was dressed in full street gear, but Macleod was used to seeing him in full regalia instead. Clearly, the man still got out on the street.

'Macleod, for God's sake, get this sorted.'

Macleod ignored the casual blasphemy. 'How secure are we here? The crime scene, everything?'

'We'll hold it. Don't worry. It won't be a problem. I'm praying for the daylight because things seem to quieten down then. It's the thing about rioting, they only enjoy it until they get tired. Then they all want to go home, put the feet up and watch Netflix for a while. I would think they'll be back out again tonight. We've got people in from Glasgow and Edinburgh up to help us, looking further afield as well. We need to get to the bottom of this.'

'I understand,' said Macleod. 'But it's not necessarily that simple.'

'I get it. But is it gang warfare?' the man asked. 'Is this a tit for tat? In which case we need to start hauling in some bodies.'

'I told the Chief Constable that I believed it was something else. It's just a feeling. Well, maybe a bit more than that.'

'Whatever it is, Macleod, we need answers, and we need them quick. Get to the bottom of it.'

Macleod put his hand out. 'Thanks for getting us in. You got plenty on your plate tonight.'

'Good luck, Seoras.'

'You too, Jim.' Macleod looked for his team but saw that they'd already disappeared around the corner of the house. As he approached it, Hope appeared holding a white coverall suit.

'Jona is in the middle of it. She says you can come in and look, but not to touch anything. It's not pretty, Seoras, even for what we see.'

Macleod nodded, took off his large raincoat, simply setting it on the floor before dressing in the white coverall outfit. Walking around the corner, he looked at a wall which had an array of spotlights on it. There was a figure there, deeply charred, and he fought back the urge to vomit at the smell of human flesh. He saw Clarissa shaking her head, almost beginning to cry.

'Clarissa, go and see if anybody saw anything.'

'Yes.'

'Keep within the circle. If you need to go anywhere, make sure somebody's with you. Go and tie up what's happened, then come back here. Okay?'

Clarissa looked at him, almost saying thank you as she walked off. Hope stood beside Macleod, much more controlled.

'He actually screwed his arms into the wall so he couldn't move.'

'It's more than one person,' said Macleod.

Jona was bending over at that point, examining something on the ground. She stood up abruptly. 'Not necessarily. Look at this.' She showed the distance of where the arms were. 'If you had two people holding him,' she said. 'Then they would have stretched his arms out further, a person can only go this far. Imagine you're having to hold one arm up, you've got a drill, a screwdriver, it's going to push through the arm. It's got to go into the wall. That takes quite a bit of force with one hand. You can hold them with the other. You may even be able to bring a knee up, something to pin him in place. You have to be reasonably strong.'

'Probably a man then,' said Macleod.

'No, that's not what I said. I said you have to be strong. There's plenty of strong women in this world.'

'How strong?' asked Macleod.

'Stronger than average,' said Hope. 'You'd have to be stronger than average to do that, Jona, wouldn't you?'

'Yes. Possibly trained as well. This isn't a youth who's done this. This isn't a group of people. Imagine, two people, you're going to hold the arms out. Three, you're going to stretch. The last thing you're going to want is the other hand to come over this way. Now, a person on their own, they're going to put the back to the free hand. They're going to incapacitate the person by possibly putting pressure up with the knee, maybe they hit them on the throat to wind them so they can't react. Then arm up quick, bang, through. Once that's done, go over and grab the other, but you're not going to stretch across them. You're going to put the arms up in a place where they can be held. You could put your hand in behind this body,' said Jona. 'You could pull that body forward, it'll still hanging. You can see he's just off the wall.'

Macleod was always astonished at Jona's detail of such macabre events, but it was her job, and she was good at it.

'So what? They stuck him up against the wall and they simply covered him in petrol and burned him?'

'No, no,' said Jona. 'Look, look around you. See all the glass bottles? There's blood on some of them. If you look at the body,' Jona reached up with gloved fingers pointing out at certain marks, 'I know there's a lot of burning and there's lot of contusions, but that body, the skin has been pierced in places. My belief, and I'll be able to confirm this when I get back into the office with him, but I think he was put up there and they're throwing bottles at him. Bottles in the ground have got blood on them. It'll be his blood, is my guess. I reckon whoever it was, they slung some of these bottles at him.'

'Then what? Doused him?'

'Yes, I think they've doused him, but also that bottle over there, that's got fuel residue on it. They're throwing a flaming bottle to set him alight.'

'But why?' asked Macleod.

'That's why they put a grenade in and they knifed him. This is like making a statement, isn't it? The others weren't? Were they?'

'Think of it,' said Hope. 'One has been knifed. There's been knifings on the estates, joyrider in a car gone up. Maybe the grenade was a statement, but he set fire to the car afterwards like joyriders do. Maybe that was the statement. This was a statement about rioters.'

Macleod bent down and looked up at the body again. 'Okay, Jona. I want you to just make sure that what you said tonight is correct. Obviously, see if you can pick up any extraneous matter, anything that might lead us to someone. Was this person tall by the way?'

'I doubt it. I can't confirm that, but I doubt it,' said Jona. 'Height of the arms, this person could be anything from about five feet five up to six feet at the most, but he could be taller. I've not lifted the man's arms up; however, given how far they are apart, and assuming a single person, I'd pitch them in about five feet seven, somewhere in that field.'

'I'll leave you to it,' said Macleod. 'Be careful. Don't go outside the area.'

'I think I can spot that,' said Jona. 'Look, I need to get this done. I want my team out of here soon. Okay? Let me get on.'

Macleod almost reeled for a moment but then realised the pressure she must have been under. Bringing a team in, a team that were not used to being in the flak. He recalled all those run-ins over the year. They'd even chased down criminals, murderers. At times, he and the team had been out in water, or arriving at deadly situations, Jona's team were there to pick up the pieces afterwards. Work out what happened. They shouldn't be working in this environment.

'Okay, Jona, you've got it. Speak later.' He turned and walked away and took off his coveralls, Hope beside him. As he put his raincoat back on, he saw Clarissa entering with a group of officers through the police cordon.

'Thanks, boys,' she said. They had a young person with them, only thirteen or fourteen, Macleod thought.

'Detective Inspector. This is Ian. He has some information. He says a lot of this, it's all been kicked off by rumours that there's gang warfare on the go.'

'Gang warfare?' asked Macleod. 'Who told you that, son?'

Ian looked up at him. The boy didn't look like he was a rioter, more someone that Macleod would have described as a scruff, bit of a rascal, and cheeky with it. Someone that might have pinched the teacher's bottom or put a tack on a chair, but he seemed to still have a bright-eyed youthfulness about him. 'What are you doing out?'

'I was out with some friends, and I can't get back now. The rioting is in the middle.'

'Have you got any folks?'

'Yes.'

'Right,' said Macleod, 'when I'm done, tell Sergeant Urquhart here their number. She'll ring them, tell them to stay put, and you stay within this ring.'

The boy actually looked relieved. Macleod thought he'd judged him correctly. 'So, what's up?' he asked. 'Why is all this kicking off?'

'Well, all the kids are saying that Peter Olive, he was killed by that guy from over in the Knockmalley gang. Words have been spoken, there's been words over these last couple of weeks. Then one of our guys threw a grenade into the car.'

'A grenade? Where did they get the grenade from?' asked

Macleod.

'Guys can get anything. They can get hold of anything, I'm telling you, all sorts of weapons. He said he's going to gear everybody up.'

'He's going to gear everyone up?' said Macleod. 'That's interesting.'

'Yes, but we're at it. We're at war, you see. I was out, out in the mansion they were all telling me this, and then the riot started. I tried to get back but then you've got your guys running down the street. We hopped off and we hid in the churchyard for a bit. Then when we came back out, I can't go across town so I stayed in the quieter bit. There is less rioting down this end. Then your sergeant here, she came over to me and started talking.'

'Have you got any friends about?' said Macleod.

'Lost them when we ran during the rioting.'

'So, you're all at war with Warmsley, are you?'

'Not me, the bigger guys and that. Said they're going to go over and do some of them.'

'Maybe you could tell Sergeant Urquhart here a few names.'

'Oh yes, grass. Grass, look I'm not telling you about people. They'll come and get me. Look at Jake. Jake Hughes had to leave; he's hiding away. You won't get me like that. I'm not doing stuff like that.'

'Okay. Have you seen any other weapons? You talk about grenades; have you seen people with knives and things like that?'

'No,' he said. 'By the way, what's that smell?'

It was the smell of human remains that have been burnt, but Macleod wasn't about to tell the kid that.

'That's just been a fire in the back. Must be some plastic or something burning. I was asking about weapons. Have you seen any of these weapons?'

'I've seen some knives and that.'

'What do they look like?' asked Macleod. Ian started drawing something in the air. He said, 'It closes up like this. Sharp blade on it, but you can put it away in your pocket.'

Macleod recognised the butterfly knife. It was far from a grenade, or the serrated edge blade that had been used on Peter Olive.

'You haven't seen anything bigger than that? They haven't shown you anything?'

'That's what they showed me. It's pretty impressive. That's why I don't tell you anything.'

'Okay. You stay here with Sergeant Urquhart.' Macleod walked away with Hope. 'I'm not buying it. I'm not buying gang warfare.'

'He talked about grenades in there, but he hasn't seen it,' said Hope. 'You could be right, Seoras.'

The pair of them walked around to the corner, standing well clear of the crime scene and the charred body of the youth who'd been attacked. 'Put him up like that single-handed,' said Macleod. 'This is a killer. A whole smoke screen running around the riots and that. We'd better cover our bases.'

'You think these riots are instigated by someone else? You think they're whipped up?'

'We'll see,' said Macleod. 'We'll see, but that there,' he said, pointing at the charred body on the wall, 'Jona says one person, strong. That's our killer, Hope. That's our killer.'

Chapter 09

Macleod stretched out, tired, but also worried. The riot through the night, down on the Walmsley Estate had taken its toll on the entire force. Macleod was a police officer, a detective, used to seeing what people could do to each other, horrific scenes of crime. But when he saw an estate alive like that, the rioting going on alongside normal homes and families, it chilled him to the bone.

It had taken a toll on the rest of the team as well. Although they'd all come back to the station, they were all quiet, sullen, not the usual banter between the team. In particular, Macleod was worried about Clarissa. She was clearly struggling after she'd been attacked and despite how well she'd handled it, Macleod could see it had upset her. Ross had seemed to cope with it better. Maybe it was in his nature to expect to be attacked. Maybe he thought because of his sexuality, it would come at different times, and he'd been mentally prepared for it.

One thing Macleod was well aware of was that they could not send any of them single-handed down to these estates again; they'd have to be prepared. He'd bought the entire team breakfast tucking into a large fry and was amazed when Hope simply had a big bowl of yoghurt with fruit. There was a reason she was probably in better shape than he.

Clarissa had picked up some bacon and toast, chewed it with a lack of enthusiasm, while Ross was maintaining his usual front, professional, polite, courteous, thanking the staff who had cooked the food. When he made his way back to his desk, Macleod had a file of photos, all showing Jai Smith and how he had died.

Single person, a single person could do that, thought Macleod. *How, what was he? Mercenary, military, some sort of trained martial artist?* But the other thing was the planning. Somebody would've had to have been driving around with this stuff, surely, or had the riot lasted long enough for them to look to make the opportunity. Whoever they were, they were clearly resourceful, able to pick a moment, spot where they could do things without anyone watching.

In the shadows, or were they in plain sight and we just couldn't see them? thought Macleod. *Were they rioting along with everyone else and then simply popped off to do their deed?* His mind swam and no wonder, he'd been up for too long.

He heard the phone ring and he ignored it at first, letting the call bounce to the outside office. He heard Ross say, 'I think he's just taking a breather. I'll put you through,' and Macleod knew who it was. He picked up the call when it rang again.

'Sorry, love,' he said, 'been a heck of a night.'

'I saw on the news. Are you okay?' asked Jane.

'I'm fine,' said Macleod. 'I'm fine. Rough night, all in. That's not even counting what we saw at the crime scene, but I'm okay.'

'What about the rest of the team?'

'Well, to be honest with you, Jane, I'm worried about Clarissa. She's finding this tough. The other two—they seem to be handling it.'

'You told me she was attacked the other day; it's no wonder she's maybe feeling vulnerable, maybe vulnerable for the first time in her life. She's quite a force.'

'She is that, but she's no Kirsten Stewart though. She wasn't brought up in a gym learning to fight.'

'No, she wasn't, Seoras; remember that. Just keep an eye on her. I'll keep an eye on you.'

'Always. I expect no less,' he said, slightly cheered at hearing Jane's voice. Macleod put the phone down and looked out the window.

Rain, we need rain, he thought. *So far, the evenings have been warm and dry; nothing better to stop a riot than some rubbish weather. Where was it when you wanted it?*

He thought back to the weather they used to get on Lewis, where he came from. The wind whipping in, the rain almost horizontal, days when you'd step outside the door and have to brace yourself to move forward or simply to stay still. They never got riots there. He'd come a long way from there, a long way.

His phone rang again and Macleod reckoned that Jane couldn't have rung back that quick so he let it ring out and then received a knock on the door from Ross.

'Sorry to bother you, sir, but that's the DCI. Apparently, Mr Mackenzie's coming back. DCI wants you up there, speak to them. Mr Mackenzie's in a foul mood, not happy with what's going on.'

'Well, Mr Mackenzie can take a running jump,' said Macleod.

'I'll not pass that on,' said Ross. 'I'm not sure it's what the

DCI's looking for.'

'Well, the DCI wouldn't be able to . . .' Macleod cut his comment short, spotting the DCI coming into the outer office.

'Seoras, get yourself together upstairs. We need to talk to these people.'

'With respect, I am running a murder investigation. We've just got in after a night out.'

'Well, I was up early as well,' said the DCI. 'Now come on. I'll expect you there in two minutes.' Macleod watched the man turn on his heel, leaving in such a dismissive fashion that Macleod's potential reaction had Ross almost running for his desk.

'It's all right, Alan. I'm not angry at you.' And then he noticed that Clarissa hadn't even offered a smug comment. Macleod walked over, saw her huddled in the chair and she began to weep.

'Easy,' said Macleod, 'easy.'

She sniffed. 'It's all right, Seoras. I'm just tired. I'm just . . . it was awful last night. Awful. Who does that to someone? Throwing fuel over them and then setting them on fire, looking to prolong their agony. It's not right.'

'Well, of course it's not right,' said Macleod. It was all he had to offer. 'Are you okay? Do you want to take the morning off, come back in later?'

Clarissa shook her head, 'And what? Have the Rottweiler go home because she's too injured?'

'I don't call you that. You know that, don't you?'

'No, but they do. And they do it because it's right; I am. Somebody's going to feel my bite with this one.'

Macleod heard Clarissa sniff hard, and as he turned away, he spied Hope in the far corner of the office, put his hand out and flicked his finger slightly to indicate she should join him outside. Once they were in the hall, Macleod turned, looking up at his tall sergeant.

'Do you think you can have a talk with her?'

'A what? Clarissa?'

'But she's struggling. I just thought you might get closer to her, you know? Being a woman and that.'

'I respect a lot of what you do, Seoras, do you know that? But see, when it comes to this whole woman-man thing, you're the most ham-fisted at times going. She's got what she needed; you dropping by. You've got a more subtle touch with her than I ever would have, but don't worry, I'll keep an eye. But how are you?'

'I'm all right. I didn't tear one apart on Ross when the DCI came in. I wouldn't have the team speak to me much when I come back from this meeting. You might find I'm not in the best frame of mind.'

He saw Hope grin briefly and then go to a sour face, realising Macleod found nothing funny about the moment. Macleod climbed the stairs up to the office of the DCI and found Simon Mackenzie and a contingent of other men and women who were introduced to him as being from the council. Macleod sat on a stool at the edge of the DCI's table while on the other end of the table sat the Assistant Chief Constable who Macleod had seen the previous night. Jim gave Macleod a nod but was very stony-faced.

'I thought it best to bring everybody in together,' said the DCI, 'so that these people from the council can get some answers from those out on the field.'

In other words, thought Macleod, *you can't even run a smoke screen. All you had to do was field all the questions while the rest*

77

of us got to work. The rest of us managed to actually deal with this situation. Instead, you brought two people in who have been up all night and get them to talk to these people who have no idea what they're on about when it comes to looking after an estate. But instead of saying all that, Macleod smiled.

'I think I speak for all of us on the council,' said Simon Mackenzie, 'when I say that we're not impressed with how you are dealing with this.'

Jim, the Assistant Chief Constable smiled, looked over at Macleod and then back towards Simon Mackenzie. 'Can I just ask what you would be advising we do?'

'You need more people. You need to go in with a tough hand. You need to suppress these kids.'

'You'd like us to run in with, what? A water canon? Big sticks? Beat them into a pulp? We're not actually sure what we're dealing with here at the moment.'

'It's clear you're dealing with a riot, a loss of control, a loss of behaviour,' said Mr Mackenzie, 'and I'm moving that we should have a task force going in to sort these people out. We need someone up at the top of that. Someone to head it up who understands police work.'

'Are you saying that I don't?' asked the Assistant Chief Constable.

'Someone maybe closer. Maybe someone closer to the street, that's what we need. Someone who understands what it is to feel that heat and that anger. Someone who people respect, see as a figurehead. Someone like Detective Inspector Macleod.'

Macleod, up until this point, had kept his eyes firmly on the floor, but raised them now, to see a gulping smile from the DCI beside him.

'Splendid. Absolutely, Seoras would make a great leader of a task force.'

'Detective Inspector Macleod is currently occupied,' said Macleod. 'I have a murder investigation on the go. The Assistant Chief Constable is absolutely correct; we don't know what's going on here. We haven't got to the root cause of it. The assumption coming from you is that it's simply antisocial behaviour that's been spiralling out of control and gone on too long. Having been out there, I'm not too sure that that's correct. However, the expert that I would seek is the Assistant Chief Constable, who, Mr Mackenzie, was out there last night in amongst all the heat and the action, and he wasn't sitting behind a police cordon like me. He was with them moving about and trying to suppress what was going on, so please, don't come in here with your high-handedness.'

'But you're still okay with the idea of being a head of a task force?' said the DCI.

Macleod turned at the man incredulous, almost muttered something but held himself back.

'I will not be head of any task force. I'm already the head of one, one that seeks to find out who was committing murders out there. Understand, we didn't just have riots, we've had six people who have been murdered, and they've been murdered with items of a serious nature. Items that are not held by the average street punk, so we'll not be reacting in some knee-jerk fashion and marching out with a poster campaign and my face all over it. When it comes to this riot, we need to take our lead from the Assistant Chief Constable; he knows what he's doing, and I trust him with my safety when I'm going into these areas. Please, I never wanted to be a poster boy, and I won't be one now.'

'But what are we going to do? We're fully expecting another

night of rioting,' said one of the councilmen.

'And so am I,' said the Assistant Chief Constable, 'and we're prepared for it. We've got people in from Aberdeen, more people up from Glasgow and Edinburgh. We're expecting two estates to try and get hold of each other, and we're going to form a wall in the middle to keep everything quiet. I'm going to do my best to allow Detective Inspector Macleod to shine a light on these murders so we can hold and back up the community and say who it wasn't. If someone's playing this area, we need to know about it.'

'In the meantime, we have shop owners who have had property destroyed.'

'And I have approximately twenty-three officers injured, and now off duty tonight. Two of them have been seriously burned. Trust me,' said the Assistant Chief Constable, 'no one is taking this more seriously than me. Now, frankly, I've been up all night, I've got a tonne of work to get on with, and I think our meeting is over.'

'You can't just fob me off like that,' said Simon Mackenzie.

Macleod stood up and began to walk for the door. 'Nobody's fobbing you off, sir,' said Macleod, 'I'm sure the Detective Chief Inspector can answer any further questions you've got.'

Macleod reached the door and held it open, allowing the Assistant Chief Constable to walk out. He closed it firmly behind him, not so everybody would think he slammed it, but in a motion that said, 'The discussion is now over.' Outside in the corridor, Jim turned to him, held out a hand.

'I know you didn't want to be in there, Seoras, but I'm mighty glad you were. Are you sure you don't want your face on a poster?' Macleod shook his head at him.

'What on earth? I remember the days when I was an officer

and nobody knew who I was except for the criminals, and that was okay because that meant you were doing your job right. Nowadays, it's all they want. I can't believe they've come to me; it's not even my field. They'll be down for Hope next.'

'I'm amazed they haven't got her up on a poster campaign already. DCI's very fond of her, I've noticed.'

'Well, heaven help him if he tried anything. She's smarter than even I can give her credit for. Anyway, I'll let you go, Jim. You've got plenty to do. I'll try and get to the bottom of this for you, quick as I can.'

'You don't need to tell me; we're two old war dogs; we know the score. We know how it can go. Do what you can, Seoras. See you later.'

Macleod watched the man walk off down the corridor, his shoulders slumped, but he actually thought there was someone with a bigger world on his shoulders than Macleod felt he had on his own.

Chapter 10

Alan Ross made contact that afternoon with a Kelly McGinley, a social worker on one of the estates, as he believed the solution to what was going on lay within the estate, and Kelly offered an opportunity to get closer to the youth. When he called her, she said that she was indeed close to them, but when she arrived at the police station, he was rather taken aback.

He reckoned she was only twenty-five at the most, wore a snug pair of jeans, had long blonde hair, and was sporting a baseball jacket. He welcomed her up into the office, taking her through the corridors of the station, and receiving the occasional turned head. Although she wasn't Ross's cup of tea, he did know what other men looked for, and clearly, Kelly would have fitted the bill. However, he'd asked her along for her expertise and to help get alongside the kids. When he sat her down at the corner of his desk, she advised that she'd been able to make a meet for that evening.

'It's all a bit fluid,' she said. 'But one of the gangs who's involved in the joy riding, he said it's okay to meet him, said there may be a few others there. It'll be over on the Knockmalley estate. He's given me one of the abandoned houses towards the far end of it. It's up to you if you want to go, Constable Ross, but it'll be the only way you'll get to talk to them unless you bring them in here. If you do that, none of them will speak; very few of them are speaking at all. They're very agitated though; four of their own have been killed. The word out in the street is it was done by the Warmsley estate.'

'And the Warmsley estate think they did in Peter Olive. Any word from the side if that was the case?

'No, absolutely none. None of them seemed to talk about Olive. A few of them might have said he'd gotten what he deserved but nobody is claiming credit for it, and I would have thought, if this was a gang thing, somebody would have claimed it, somebody would have put themselves out there as the hero of the hour, but there's nothing.'

'What about Jai Smith?'

'Jai Smith is a name that hasn't been on our estate.'

'Who was he?'

'He looks like a kid that's got caught up,' said Kelly McGinley. 'I talked to my fellow social worker over on the Warmsley Estate, and he said Jai wasn't that bad a kid. "They were the bad crowd," he said. 'That happens sometimes.'

'One thing if we're going over,' said Ross, 'it'd probably be best if you call me Alan, certainly not constable; there's no need to keep reminding them, throwing it in their faces.'

'No, but they know you're a copper. I didn't hide that from them. There's no way I can go in with a copper on my elbow and not say it. I had to work hard at getting them to agree to this, so make of it what you will. I also can't guarantee your safety.'

Ross looked over at the woman. 'Really?' he said. 'That bad.'

'I wouldn't guarantee my own, so yes, that bad.'

'If you can't guarantee our safety, then I need to talk to the boss,' said Ross. 'In fact, come with me.' Ross led Kelly over to Macleod's office, where he knocked on the door. There was a brief hello and Ross opened the door and saw Macleod sitting down at the conference desk with Hope, going through various bits of evidence.

'I need your permission to do something, boss,' said Ross. 'This is Kelly McGinley; she's a social worker on the Knockmalley estate. She can get me into a meeting with a lot of the young people, some who were friends with the joyriders. They're looking for answers, but I might be able to ask some questions as well. Unfortunately, she says that she can't guarantee my safety.'

Macleod stood up, walked around from the table, and put a hand out to Kelly McGinley. 'Detective Inspector Seoras Macleod.'

'I know,' said Kelly. 'I've seen you on the television.' Macleod almost rolled his eyes. He shook her hand anyway.

'I'm glad you're trying to help us. However, Ross's comment makes me feel a little uneasy. When you say, you can't guarantee his safety, what do you mean by that? Can you guarantee your own?'

'I would normally be all right. I've announced him as a copper before I've gone in. Sorry, police officer. It's always copper when you talk to the kids. They know I'm good. They know I won't grass them up. They know that anything they say to me doesn't go further, and it has to be like that; otherwise, I can't work with them.'

'So, if I said to you, have they said anything regarding any of these murders, you wouldn't reply to me anyway if they had?'

'Well, actually in this case,' said Kelly, 'I can reply to you.

84

With regards to any of them being involved in any of the killings, there's been absolutely no talk of it. None. As I said to Constable Ross, that would seem strange. I would expect them to boast. It would be an extreme measure to go and kill someone but with the way the riots have been recently, and everything else going on, it just seems to be different now. There seems to be a bigger edge to them, a bigger edge to everything. Residents are scared, too.'

'Well, that's not surprising. It's mainly been on the Warmsley estate at the moment,' said Macleod, 'but they reckon Knockmalley's looking like it's going to take off as well. The Assistant Chief Constable's planning for that.'

'Then that's probably very wise,' said Kelly.

'I think it's important I go and do this though, boss, but given the comment of Ms McGinley, I thought it worthwhile to mention it to you.'

Macleod looked over at Hope. 'There's your line manager,' said Macleod. 'What do you think?'

'I'd rather you went in with a lot more people, Alan,' said Hope.

'Then you wouldn't get in,' said Kelly. 'I said one and I said with me. I'm hoping it'll be okay if I'm there.' Hope gave a grim nod to Macleod.

'Well, take care. First sign of trouble, get out. I'm going to ask the Assistant Chief Constable to put a van in a nearby location, so if they have to come for you, they can. Take a panic button. Something you can set off.'

'They'll search for that.'

'He'll need his phone.'

'That's about all he'd be able to have.'

'It seems they accept phones,' said Macleod

85

'Everybody has a phone, don't they?' replied Kelly

'Okay, thanks,' said Macleod. 'Set it up with quick download on something you can reach us. Set up some sort of panic signal.' Ross nodded and asked Ms McGinley to leave the room with him.

That evening, at approximately seven-thirty, Ross was led in to an abandoned house, along with Ms McGinley. Stepping inside, he saw it was dark until a couple of candles were lit, and he suddenly realised that they were far from alone. He clocked at least twenty faces.

'Is this him?' said a voice at the front. Ross turned to see a clean-shaven man, maybe of about nineteen, whose hair was cropped extremely short. He was carrying a knife in one hand, and Ross did his best not to show any emotion. Beside him was a girl. Her face looked full of thunder.

'What's his name?'

'Alan,' said Ross. 'My name's Alan. Detective Constable, Inverness Police Station.'

'Is this it, Kelly?' the man said to the social worker. Kelly nodded, moved away from Ross and sat down almost like an intermediate distance between the two men. 'This is Scarlet with me,' said the boy. 'Her sister died when they killed her in the car.'

'I'm sorry for that,' said Ross.

'We don't want you to be sorry. We want to know who the hell did it. Why haven't you gone for them yet?'

'We haven't gone for them because we don't know who did it yet.'

'The Warmsley lot, wasn't it? That Warmsley lot.'

'Is that what you think?' asked Ross. 'What evidence have you got for that?'

'We don't need evidence, do we?'

'Somebody didn't,' said Ross. 'Jai Smith died last night. Somebody screwed his arms to a wall, threw a load of fuel over and set him on fire.' Ross scanned the faces around him. There was shock amongst them, and then there was a grin from some people.

'But he probably deserved it.'

'Did you know him? Jai Smith. Did anybody here actually even know him? Apparently, he didn't deserve this. Just out with a riot. Just running with the crowd from what I can gather.'

'Who told you that, copper?'

He nodded towards Kelly. 'Kelly's got her counterpart with her working on that estate. He said it.'

'They'd say anything.'

'What? Like Kelly would? She won't tell me any secrets, but she's protective of you lot. I think she knows you,' said Ross.

'I don't care what she knows. I want you. I want to know what you know.' A knife was pulled from the inner jacket of several of those around, and Ross found himself suddenly being circled, knives being waved. 'You're going to tell me what you know.'

'I'll tell you what I know,' said Ross. 'Somebody put a grenade in a car over here, killed four of you in that car before setting it on fire. They pulled up in a car beside it. Grenades just don't come in the streets. I mean, you guys, you're not going to have grenades.'

Ross threw the carrot out there and suddenly the knives were being put away.

'No,' said the leader, 'but I've got one of these.' And he pulled a gun from his jacket. Ross looked around. Nobody else pulled a weapon. Nobody else showed a gun.

'Just the one,' said Ross.

'One's enough, isn't it?' He walked forward putting the gun into Ross's face.

'One that would be a major mistake. You might kill me, but you guys would be the ones who'd suffer for it. You had us come out to this abandoned house, but they'll know where we are. They're all over the estate now, people you can't see. You kill me, they'll come for you, and they'll come for you big time. You've never seen a police force work until they're after the killer of one of their own. You'll also leave Kelly here scarred for life, but you've also told me one thing; you haven't got the fire power to do what they did to you.'

'We could do anything to them.'

'No, you couldn't,' said Ross.

'Could do anything to you, copper.'

'Like I've said, that would be an incredibly stupid move.'

'You're very smug,' he said. 'You have no idea what it's like here. We've got no opportunities. Nothing.'

'And you're assuming that I grew up with every opportunity? You have no idea what it was like to be me,' said Ross. 'No idea what I suffered.' He saw the guy looking completely blank at him.

'You tell me, though. You tell me who killed our lot. You step forward.' The gun now right in Ross's face.

'No,' said Ross. 'If I even knew I wouldn't tell you. I'm a copper, but I'll tell you this. If we did know who did it, we would have arrested them by now. We wouldn't hang about on this. I'm afraid we don't know, but I'll tell you what I do know. It's probably not the gang on the Warmsley Estate because if they're as badly equipped as you, they're not capable.'

'You better get this scum out of here, Kelly. He's annoying me.'

Ross stood up. He turned to go, but then turned back around. 'What's the biggest blade you've got?' he asked.

'What?' said the guy.

'What's your best blade? Show me your best blade.' There was some confusion. Then after a few minutes, a couple of knives were laid down in front of Ross. There was a large butterfly knife, impressive item, but no serrations on it like the knife that had killed Peter Olive. 'Thank you,' said Ross. 'You guys didn't do anything on that estate and I suspect they didn't do anything here.'

Ross walked out. Outside, he heard Kelly running after him. 'That was incredibly brave,' she said. She put an arm on his shoulder, then reached down for his hand. Ross looked at her.

'No, it wasn't. They're just kids and they're scared, and I don't blame them. They haven't got the ammunition to go up with whoever killed their four. They were hoping I would know, and I don't. Unfortunately, this is as bad as my boss thought it is. He's worried, worried this isn't just some sort of an estate matter. Something else is going on.'

'But, whatever I can do to help. You said something about growing up. You said that you understood, that you had the hard life, too. What estate did you grow up on?'

'No estate,' said Ross. 'Trouble was, I wasn't like all the other boys, and that was back in the day when you couldn't say it. They're in a culture of fear trying to be something they're not. I get that. I truly get that.'

Chapter 11

Macleod sat in his office awaiting his team's arrival. He had called a conference for that evening after Ross got back from the estate. He was very aware that there could be another night of rioting and had the news on his TV screen while awaiting the arrival of his team. Hope was first through the door, carrying two cups of coffee.

Macleod was very aware that they always brought him coffee. Clarissa said it was necessary unless you wanted a crank chairing the meeting. He found himself letting a lot more things go, quips and comments than he ever used to. Back in the day nobody would've called him cranky, never mind a subordinate. Of course, they weren't subordinates anymore; it was one big team, one happy family, as the DCI said. With the exception of the DCI, that might even be true.

Jona Nakamura struggled in a few minutes after Hope, the demure Asian woman looking professional as ever, but Macleod could see the strain on her. Whenever she was on scene, no matter how heinous the crime, Jona always looked like it was all a matter of a day's work. You never saw the moments when she stepped aside. Macleod put it down to her meditation, the way in which she handled herself, taking time out to ease the pain, as she'd put it to him. He'd gone on these sessions before with her, but it never seemed to be as successful with him.

Maybe there was a mindset in there as well. She'd come from a different world background; was that it? But Jona had grown up in the UK so Macleod didn't know, and that was okay. These days, more and more things he didn't seem to know.

Trundling in a few minutes later, Clarissa Urquhart swept her shawl off her shoulders, throwing it onto the coat stand in the corner of the main office before bustling her way through. Macleod always thought she was like some sort of bull in a china shop; storming in here, there, and wherever, but he'd also grown very affectionate towards her. Not only because she'd recently saved his life, but also because she was good for the team and kept him on his toes.

She spoke to him in a way Hope never would. Even though he hoped one day that his senior sergeant would; maybe then, she'd be ready. Maybe then, he could go quit all this for Jane. Who was he kidding? It was in his blood and 'justice for all' rang through his head. That was how Jane described him at times, but he never saw himself as that—some sort of avenging angel. He was just there to tidy up the pieces; pieces that often didn't fit back together because no matter what happened, people were always left wounded.

He thought about the rioting. True, they could clean up all the glass, but somebody always felt something because of it; Jai Smith's parents for a start; that was a life gone. A family broken, ruined. There were four others in that car and then again, there was Peter Olive.

He watched the television. Some people were saying that

these young people had deserved it, but Macleod could never accept that people deserved to be murdered, never; it cut against a bone. There was a lot of things you could do wrong in life, but murdering people was beyond appeal.

It was almost nine o'clock when Ross arrived, approximately twenty minutes late. He opened the door, clearing his throat. 'Apologies, sir. I think it took a little bit longer than I thought.'

'Did you get anywhere?' asked Macleod.

'Let him get a seat first of all, Seoras, for goodness sake.' There it was, Clarissa chipping in. Hope, however, had stood up, made her way round the table, and walked past Ross out to where the coffee was, pouring him a cup. Ross went to fuss after her, but Clarissa told him to sit down.

'How did it go?' asked Macleod. 'Did you learn anything?'

'I learned it's not them; definitely not them. There's no gang war going on here, at least not yet. The way things are going though, there soon could be one.'

'How do you mean?' asked Macleod.

'Well,' said Ross, taking a seat and accepting his coffee from Hope, clutching two hands around it, 'you see, they're all very big on bravado. I went in there and Kelly had to go and sit away from me. They're circling around, some of them brandishing knives showing them to me, lording it over me and having a go at me, asking me who killed their people. Of course, I don't know, so I just talked to them straight.'

'They pulled a knife on you?' asked Macleod. 'You should have run them in.'

'No, he shouldn't,' said Clarissa, 'he wouldn't have had any respect for that. What did you do, Alan?'

'Well, I tried to talk to them. I tried to see it from their point of view, and I tried to put forward from our point of view, but

I also tried to entice out of them what sort of weapons they had. They had one gun between them. To be honest, it didn't look that powerful. When he held it up to my head . . . '

'He held it where?' roared Macleod.

'To my head. It's just a show of strength, nothing really. They're scared. They're running scared.'

'Maybe,' said Clarissa, 'but I don't run scared and beat some people up or start throwing bottles around.'

'Because you know not to. What do you do when you get scared?' asked Ross.

'I watch out; I stand my ground.'

'And you put your dukes up,' said Macleod. 'That's the poetic way of putting it, isn't it?' Clarissa stuck her tongue out at him.

'The Inspector's right though,' said Ross. 'You stand there. You grit your teeth. You show them you can't be bullied. You can't be pushed aside. That's all they're doing, but they're doing it in the language they understand—guns, bottles, whatever.'

'You're not saying they haven't got anything to be blamed for, are you?' asked Hope.

'Of course not,' said Ross, 'there's plenty of opportunities. There's plenty of things to go and do. There's plenty of things more than just hanging out. Plenty of things to make a start on.'

'Speaking of weapons,' said Jona, 'what was the biggest knife they had?'

'Oh, it was a splendid butterfly knife, no serrated edges. Many of them got their knives out. There's nothing even vaguely equivalent to what you were talking about on the Peter Olive murder.'

'I still think it's military issue,' said Jona, 'serrations, definitely; big, fat, chunky, hard to use. Once again in and out, in and out, in and out, butchering him like someone who knew what to do.'

'But if they knew what to do, it would be in, cut, job done, and dusted,' said Clarissa.

'Yes,' said Macleod, 'except maybe he didn't want it to look like that. Maybe he wanted it to look like a hack and slash. Maybe he wanted to appear to be somebody else. The trouble is, somebody else hacking and slashing, might not have killed him at all, or they might have simply have killed him straight away. This person wanted him to suffer.'

'That's correct,' said Jona, 'and he would have suffered; he'd have suffered greatly. He'd have seen who was killing him as well.'

'Have we found any connection between Peter Olive and Jai Smith? Or even between our other four; anything from that angle, Ross?'

'No, nothing. What I do know is that there's been agitation going on around the estate, something's whipping this up. I'm not sure it's coming from either side.'

'What's your evidence for that?' asked Macleod.

'I don't have it completely, it's a feeling, just talking to them, they kept saying, it was the other side this, the other side that's causing them to react, like they hadn't reacted before. There are two dead in the Walmsley Estate. We had four gone up in that car; you think they'd be at it fully at this point. It makes no sense.'

'No, it doesn't,' said Hope. 'If we go after these young people, we'll be going after the wrong person.'

'That's my feeling, too,' said Macleod, 'but how do we reach in to get the other? What have we got? The third murder, Jona. Did you get anything from the crime scene?'

'I got you a rough height. I told you they were professional, I told you they were strong. I thought I did pretty well with that.'

'Well, of course you did,' said Macleod, 'it wasn't meant as a slate, but was there anything beyond that?'

'No hair, no fabric, nothing like that. The fuel poured on him, you can get just about anywhere. The bottle had the same fuel inside it, lit with a rag. No idea where that was from; it went up anyway and it was burnt—very well done.'

'And very coolly done,' said Macleod. 'You have an estate that's in the middle of a riot and he managed to single aside one person.'

'How do you do that?' said Hope. 'How do you know he's going to be there? How do you know Jai Smith is going to run down that side of the house?'

'You don't,' said Macleod. 'Jai Smith's a random victim.'

'How do you mean?' asked Hope.

'Jai Smith wasn't seen as anyone in particular on the estate, was he?'

'No,' said Ross, 'talking to Kelly McGinley, and she spoke to her co-social worker who works on the Walmsley Estate, and he said Jai Smith was not a bad kid, yeah, boisterous and all that and getting stuck into things that he shouldn't have, but no more, no worse than anyone else.'

'But he's part of the crowd,' said Macleod. 'They have a riot; you're going to know one of the crowd is going to split; somebody's got to run off.'

'And if you know where the crowd is going, if you know whereabouts, you could be prepped,' said Clarissa.

'So, we're looking at someone that can operate tidy, operate also with a plan, but a plan that can adapt, because while

95

you think someone's going to come down there, it's not guaranteed.'

'What's to stop them being out tonight?' asked Ross. 'What's to stop tonight being another death? What's to stop them going over to the Walmsley or whipping up a riot in Knockmalley? I think I want to go back out tonight, I've got a few of the faces now in my head.'

'What? Just wander the street?' said Macleod. 'We'll have to gear you up for a start. Better going out on the bus with the boys and girls from downstairs.'

'No, he's not,' said Clarissa, 'Alan wants to be out there; he wants to read it.'

'Well, I'll go then,' said Macleod.

'You can't,' said Clarissa.

'But I can't put him out there either, can I?' Macleod shot Clarissa a look, 'It's not safe; no, Alan.'

'Sir, we need to understand, we need to be out and about and catch a glimpse of what's really happening. You can't do it, your face is too well known, Sergeant McGrath the same, I'm not. With all due respect, Clarissa, you'd stand out a mile.'

'And with all due respect,' said Clarissa, 'there's no way in hell I am going to stand out there in the middle of that nonsense, not as sprite as I used to be.'

It was the first time Macleod had ever heard Clarissa put herself down, especially in front of a large group.

'If you're going to go out, Alan, undercover, but no risks, keep away from things. It's an observation exercise only and if needs be, get inside a house, flash the badge, get in, get off the street. You can ring us, and we can come and get you.'

'Okay, if that's the conditions we operate under.'

'You could take somebody out with you,' said Macleod.

'No,' said Ross, 'I can't. I can't take any of you for the reasons I've just said. I don't want to take out somebody who's just along for the ride and being instructed to do it. I need everybody that can get out there policing the riot normally, and besides, on my own, I could operate quicker. I wouldn't have to be looking out for a partner, easier to get myself off the street and just go.'

'Okay,' said Macleod, 'we'll discuss it further, but you can go. Anybody got anything else to contribute?'

'One problem I've got,' said Hope; 'they're leaving the bodies, it's not like it's a massive statement.'

'How much of a statement do you need to make?' asked Macleod.

'Well,' said Hope, 'the thing is, if we had a serial killer with that last death, that'd have been put up everywhere; he'd have made a deal of it.'

'But he didn't,' said Macleod, 'In fact, we did well to find the poor kid. The first one just looks like a random knife stabbing. The second one, if you didn't know about the grenade, you would have said the car crashed.'

'But the grenade was necessary,' said Jona; 'without it, they couldn't be sure everybody in that car was dead. Chances of anyone surviving the grenade were very little. They also then couldn't move when they poured all the fuel over the car.'

'Why not simply run up and put a bullet in everybody?' said Ross.

'Because then it doesn't look like something from the estate,' said Clarissa. 'A grenade, yes, it's a bit extravagant, but, you know, it's just tossed into the car, and then everything goes up.'

'So, somebody's setting everything up. I need to know where.

Jona, any luck with that grenade? Have you got the details of it?'

'I have indeed. I think it's British Army, or at least the British Army is one of the people that uses it. I've got the specs here.'

'I'll run that through,' said Ross. 'Pass it to me, Jona, I'll see what I can find.'

'Let me give them a quick ring first, ask them if they lost one.'

'They are hardly going to admit to that, losing lethal weapons, especially when someone's dead,' said Ross.

'Well, if they don't, pretty soon they're going to be in here helping us with the riots. Trace it,' said Macleod. 'Soon as you're back off the street, trace it.' Macleod dismissed the team, then made his way over to the window. He didn't look towards either estate; instead, it showed a rather peaceful residential side of Inverness and there were lights on in homes.

'You wanted to see me before I went out, sir,' said Ross.

'You got a reason for doing this?' said Macleod. 'Because if you do, I want to know it now. If you're banking for promotion, this won't earn you it. If you're trying to impress me, you did that years ago. Why on earth are you sticking your neck out like this?'

'Because I get them,' said Ross. 'I get these kids. I don't condone what they do, but I understand them. They're afraid, very afraid so, therefore, they arm themselves up. They try and put a show of strength out. I get it, I really do, and I just want to help them.'

'Fair enough,' said Macleod. 'Remember, stay back, observation only. If things go wrong, get inside a house. Shut yourself up tight. We'll come get you when it's quiet.'

'Yes, sir.' Ross turned around and went to make for the door.

'Oh, and, Alan,' said Macleod.

'Yes, sir.'

'Would you call me Seoras for once?'

'Yes, sir. Seoras, sir. Will do, sir.' Ross left the room, and a wide grin came across Macleod's face.

Chapter 12

Ross had borrowed one of Hope's leather jackets but still felt somewhat small while wearing it. He didn't realise what a frame she truly had. She was taller than him but she had a broadness with it, not one that made her look unfeminine but one that just fitted into the natural size of the woman.

She wasn't big on perfumes for which Ross was thankful. The jacket complimented the scrubby jeans and boots he was wearing along with a t-shirt that had last been aired over ten years ago. He didn't even recognize the rock band that was on it.

Currently, he was on the Knockmalley estate which tonight was seething. Everywhere he looked, young people were on the streets. More than that, he swore he could see older people too, disaffected, angry, and he wondered where they'd all been previously.

Some residents had come out to protest against those that were causing all the trouble. The police had already broken up various spats. Ross had kept himself out of the way trying to make sure that none of the local force spotted him. The baseball cap that was half pulled down over his face allowed for it. Ross also carried a quarter of whisky in his pocket or so it would seem to anyone who was looking at it. The cold tea he had replaced the whisky with didn't taste great but if he had to, he could soon down it in front of someone looking like a bit of a drunkard.

He moved with a shuffle, shambling along to give the impression of fragility and generally causing a lot of people to give him a wide berth. The young people didn't want to know him, old alcoholic. The older people passed him by except for one or two others who'd come looking to take his alcohol off him. Ross gave the grump impression and it scared off a couple and then plonked himself down here and there around the estate, like it was just too much energy to go anywhere else.

He saw Kelly McGinley walk past and she completely failed to spot who he was. Yes, she had reached forward with a kindly hand, but he'd waved her off. He then saw her go and talk to some of the young people, pleading with a lot of them to go back indoors, to stay off the streets tonight. It was a kindly thing to do because, in all honesty, she should get herself off the street, but Ross felt she was someone with a heart for the children and that's what they were, weren't they? He always used the word 'youth' but most of these youths were just still kids.

Kids with bodies approaching adulthood. Ones that could do more damage. They ran around like little toddlers and Ross found some of the attitudes incredible. They were nowhere near ready to be let loose in the big world.

Without having any kids of his own, Ross always thought about what it would be like. His work kept him busy, and his partner Angus had his own work and so there never seemed to be the time. And then some others would balk at the idea of the pair of them bringing up any child.

That wasn't what bothered Ross; what bothered him, he felt, was what bothered most wannabe parents. 'How would my life be disturbed? It'll be thrown upside down,' and as a detective constable, he didn't keep good hours. That was all right for Angus, but would he want to be the motherly figure at home?

Ross was snapped back to his senses by the appearance of Simon Mackenzie. He was surrounded by a number of cameras and was clearly giving his take on what was happening around him. Ross thought it was brave of him to be out amongst it and he could see a number of police officers thinking it unwise. The camera crews were generally safe. After all, if you're causing a riot you wanted to make sure there was somebody there to tell everybody else about it. A lot of them were hardened reporters anyway.

Reporters were streetwise, having spent many years out and about reporting on trouble. They knew where to get a good scoop but they also saw when things were going pear-shaped and they needed to stand at a distance. Like his colleagues, he didn't get to step out of the way, only into the fray when things went wrong.

Ross staggered to his feet, or at least pretended to, and shuffled his way over, so he was near Simon Mackenzie, able to hear the man speak.

'So, what in your opinion, Mr Mackenzie, is the real reason for the riots we're surrounded by at the moment?' The newspaper reporter placed a microphone in Mackenzie's face and the man smiled and then gave a worried impression.

'The blame quite literally is with the people here. I'm not talking about those who have come out to try and calm things down. I'm talking about those who seem intent on causing destruction within their own place. Those who want to destroy that which they live amongst. We've had an increase in joyriding, an increase in stabbings, in general maliciousness, and despite the good work of several on these estates, it's being tarnished at every turn.

'The kids that don't go to school, kids that don't go to jobs, people that just want to take, well, we've had enough of it. We really have. I'm calling for a task force to come in here. I'm calling for those who crack down on the lawbreakers in our land to come in and sweep these people off the streets. Why should they get to run amok? Why should they see girlfriends getting accommodation, then living off the benefits? Why? There are good people on this estate. People that have worked hard all their life, struggling to get by, to make ends meet. I say they should sweep in here and just eradicate these spongers. If they don't want to look after the houses they're given, throw them out.'

'You're advocating putting them on the street,' said another reporter.

'Some of them should be locked up, never mind on the street, or maybe some sort of forced labour where they can pay for their accommodations.'

'That's quite an extreme measure. You think that'll be popular with your voters?'

'I represent the decent people in Inverness, those who don't want trouble like this. Our city is flourishing. We have new estates going up on the edges where people come in and they take up jobs and they contribute to our community. It's thriving and then we have backward estates like this where we have kids out of control running amok. Kids that . . . '

Ross saw the item from a distance. It was a bottle, small, looked like a quarter of whisky. There was still liquid inside it but the arc it was flying on was clearly going to land on Simon Mackenzie's head. Ross watched him turn as the bottle arrived closer and it clocked him just above the forehead. There was a crack, and the next thing Ross saw was blood streaming down the face of Simon Mackenzie.

Part of him wanted to run forward, start to deal with the situation, make sure the man didn't put his hand too close in case any glass had lodged. He wanted to call for an ambulance, put something around the wound, compress it and keep the blood from coming out, but Ross was undercover and he didn't want to break it now. There was no way the character he was playing would be able to deal with a situation like this. He'd be rumbled straight away.

Ross watched as the man stepped here and there in front of the cameras, blood pouring from his head and then a paramedic ran up, leading him away, but not before Simon Mackenzie stopped. 'This is why we need him. We need the likes of Macleod.'

Ross swallowed hard. The boss wasn't going to like that. He never wanted to be up in the public eye. That wasn't what the Inspector was about. The Inspector was about solving cases, putting people behind bars because they'd done wrong. Keeping them off the street, keeping them from killing other people.

Simon Mackenzie was led away to an ambulance, followed all the while by the TV crews, at least until the next shout came up; the community hall had been put on fire. Ross stumbled along, so he was close to it. Mixing among kids running back and forward, he could hear them shouting. 'Who did that?

Who put that up?' But nowhere did he get an answer.

He looked around to see what a lot of them were carrying. Yes, there were some stones and bottles, but to set somewhere alight, how had they done it? It wasn't that easy to get a fire going somewhere, unless you had fuel to throw over, or you could cause some sort of explosion. *Had they turned on gas? Wasn't the usual way it was done. After all, gas was risky; you couldn't see it and you didn't know where it was. You could set fire to something and end up blowing yourself up in the process.* He staggered along and bumped accidentally into a lad who turned around and looked at him.

'What are you doing, Grandad?'

Inside Ross, smiled. The greyish hair and the wig must have done wonders along with the fake beard.

'What's happening, son? What's that light over there?'

'They set the community hall on fire?'

'Who?' asked Ross.

'I don't know. We were all over on the other side and then the community hall went on fire.'

'Where do we go? Where do we go to next?' asked Ross.

'You're in the riot? Good Lord. You'll see some of them, some of the older men, they're telling us what to do. It's good that it's organised. I think that's what's happening. We're pushing the police from one place, then we're dragging them to the other. I've hit a couple of them with some bottles tonight.'

Part of Ross wanted to reach out, grab the kid and tell him to stop being so stupid, to get inside, but what worried the man more was his talk of older men also being on the estates where the kids that were causing trouble. The kids were eighteen at the most, seventeen, sixteen, fifteen. They weren't older men. Where'd they come from?

105

The young lad saw a policeman coming towards them and he hobbled off.

'He causing you any problems?'

'No,' said Ross and recognised Ian Carson. He'd worked a bit with Ross for several years, but the man's face showed no recognition. 'Just getting my way home, Officer,' said Ross. He stopped briefly, taking out the bottle and drinking a little bit of the cold tea that was inside.

'You probably want to put that away, sir,' said Carson. 'How far are you from home?'

'Three corners. I'll get there. Don't you worry. You go and stay with that fire,' said Ross. Carson looked at him, gave a shake of the head, and walked off back to his duties. Ross did anything but go around the next two corners. Instead, he followed the crowd as they seemed to migrate over towards the community hall on fire.

He watched as youths threw bottles, but behind them was a line of older men. The kids would come back, one would get told something and they'd race out telling the others what to do. *There is organisation behind this*, Ross thought. *Organisation on a level that doesn't make sense.* He saw Kelly McGinley again, a number of the older lads around her.

He understood why she would enthral them, could grab their attention without even trying, overactive hormones making them look like a desperate crowd around a charlatan's roadshow. *Maybe I should have brought Hope in,* he thought. *She might have got more out of the teenagers.*

Ross stifled a laugh, watching as Kelly managed to get a couple of the younger lads to head off home. Ross looked to his left and saw a line of police officers. As if from nowhere, bottles started being thrown, Molotov cocktails lighting up the night as they crashed onto the floor, cracking onto the ground, spilling their contents across it, which then ignited, pouring flames at the feet of the police officers.

He saw them getting ready to charge, to break up the crowd and Ross stepped around the corner of the block he was on. He stepped inside the stairs of a group of flats. Slowly, he climbed up three floors to a position where he could look down on the crowd and pretend to stand there supping on his quart of whisky. From his vantage point, he could see the charge, the young people breaking up, but then only streets away being reformed. He watched as bottles, stones, anything else, got launched into the crowd of police officers. There were a number of residents still on the street running out of the way, but once the situation had moved onto other streets, Ross returned and followed it.

He spent the next two hours moving round the estate, flash point after flash point. He saw cars being set alight, a couple of chairs being thrown about, and then he saw a single house. The one beside it was boarded up, and there were a number of youths at the door banging on it, shouting for whoever was inside.

Ross pretended to stumble across the street towards it. His face was in horror when he saw a couple of youths pull an old woman out through the door, charging inside. He walked over to the house and found her sitting down on the cold ground outside. She could have been eighty or ninety and she was in tears. Ross looked around him, but there was a line further up where the police were fighting with the local youths in the riot. One of the young people, who had gone up to the house, exited with a TV set in his hands.

'Where are you going with that?' asked Ross.

'There's plenty in there, man. Go and get what you want.'

'Put it back,' said Ross.

'Piss off, drunkard,' said the young lad. 'I want a turn.'

Ross put his hand on the kid's shoulder. 'I said, "Put it back."'

The kid put the TV down, turned to Ross, and reached for his pocket, pulling out a knife.

'You going to make me?'

Ross didn't wait. He grabbed the kid's wrist, squeezing it so hard that the knife fell from his hand. He then pulled him towards him and drove a knee into his stomach before pinning him on the floor. A couple of his mates ran out of the house, and Ross piled into them, cracking one with a punch to the jaw, causing the blood to flow from one side. Another he threw into the wall of the house before kicking him in the backside, telling him to get the hell out. Another two looked up in horror and ran. He stood his ground, watching them go, daring them not to come back.

The old lady was still on the floor, crying. He bent over and picked her up before taking her back inside her house and sitting her down on the sofa. He then stepped outside and retrieved the TV, setting it up where he thought it was in the living room and switching it on for coverage of the riots. He locked her front door, moving a dresser across it. He then locked the back as well.

After making a cup of tea for the old lady, he watched her drink it, checked her over to make sure that she didn't have any lasting damage. He told her he would sit downstairs while she went off to bed. She probably wouldn't sleep, and he'd place a call in to make sure the police dropped in on her the following morning, but he wouldn't tell the inspector or any of the others about this. After all, he delivered some good hits on those kids As he sat watching the riots on the TV, Ross had the overwhelming feeling that there was something else going on behind the air of social disruption.

Chapter 13

Macleod sat watching the television, scanning to see if he could see Ross. Wherever he was in Hope's leather jacket, it must have been a good disguise because Macleod couldn't spot him anywhere. The inspector prided himself on attention to detail, but he also had a sense of pride that Ross was blending in so well. He had serious concerns about what Ross was doing, but they needed to get to the bottom of what was happening out there.

So far, they'd almost no link to who the actual killer or killers were. If they had indeed come from the estates, there would be things left behind that would say so, or else the bragging rights giving away those who couldn't keep their mouths shut about what they'd done. Macleod thought everything was too well planned and too well executed. Maybe if they pulled them into some sort of kangaroo court, did them over, and then threw them out onto the street as a comment, Macleod might have thought it was a completely out-of-control estate.

But everything that Ross had said indicated that they were scared young people looking to defend themselves but certainly not out to kill. Unfortunately, things like that could change, especially if the wrong people were behind them, influencing them. Today with the social media channels, it was too easy for things to get blown up out of all proportion. Word of mouth was always a good thing because it never spread as quick as a Twitter feed or an Instagram post. He wasn't too sure if any of these kids used Facebook these days. That made him feel especially old.

There was a light cough from the office outside and Macleod looked up to see Clarissa Urquhart standing up and almost doubling over. His first thought was to race through the door and see if she was all right, but then he clocked that somebody was coming in through the main office door, out beyond his own. With that amount of reaction from Clarissa, it could only mean one thing. Macleod wondered did he have time to hide in the office to pretend he was out? Could he grab his jacket and run past him? The DCI would be annoyed, but Macleod could take his anger any day, better than any words he had to say. As the thoughts raced through Macleod's head, he noticed that the DCI had somebody with him.

There was no knock on Macleod's door. It simply opened, and the DCI marched in with Simon Mackenzie in his wake. The man's head was bandaged in a way that made him look like Mr Bump, and Macleod stifled a laugh.

'Did you see it?' said the DCI. 'Did you see what happened to Mr Mackenzie?'

'Simon, please,' said Mackenzie, 'just Simon.'

'Did you fall over, Mr Mackenzie?' asked Macleod with a completely straight face.

'Have you not been watching the riots?' said the DCI. 'It's all over. Look.' Macleod found his TV screen being switched to some other channels. He had indeed been watching the riots, and currently the TV was on the ad break, but his boss

111

switched over to the other channel that ran without ads and sure enough, they were showing a replay of Mr Mackenzie getting hit on the head.

'That was quite some shot,' said Macleod.

'Disgraceful is what it is,' said the DCI. 'It's disgraceful. I was just going to get the .Assistant Chief Constable. We need to get a plan together. We need to get things in motion.'

'I thought the Assistant Chief Constable did have it in motion. Jim's good at what he does,' said Macleod. 'I'd leave Jim to it.'

'No, we need a figurehead. We need a face at the front and you're the face for that,' said the DCI. Macleod didn't turn around from the television. Instead, watching it, he saw lines of police having to run in with riot shields, breaking up several youths throwing bottles and stones.

'I don't think a trusted face is going to do much for you there.'

'That's where you're wrong, Inspector Macleod, or can I call you Seoras?'

'Inspector Macleod's fine.'

'Well, Inspector, to have you in the front, the public know who you are. They know what you do. You always get your man or woman, and they need some belief that we're going to sort this situation out.'

'Jim will sort the situation out,' said Macleod. 'The Assistant Chief Constable is on it, and I for one will give him every backing. He's asked me to find out who committed these murders, and that's what I'll do. I don't need to be distracted by being some sort of poster boy.'

'I think poster boy is a little bit excessive. You're more than that. You're an icon.'

Macleod raised his eyes as Mackenzie said it. The door was

open behind out into the other office, and Macleod was sure that the remainder of his team could hear what was being said. This was confirmed when Clarissa suddenly snorted as if the coffee had gone down the wrong way, but Macleod knew what had set her off.

'I'll give you a direct order,' said the DCI.

'No,' said Macleod. 'This is not our field, not what we're doing. The Assistant Chief Constable is the one to make decisions like this. If he says he wants me up on a poster, I'll do it for him.'

'I'm your boss. You'll do it for me.'

'No,' said Macleod, and he turned, his face looking like thunder. 'No. We have a killer to catch. Now, if you're not going to be any use, with all due respect, get out.'

The DCI's face was livid and red. He stood for a moment, looking at Macleod who wondered if he'd overstepped the mark, but the man had deserved it. The Assistant Chief Constable would back Macleod up on his decision. He might take him into the office and tell him to calm down a bit and not to speak in such a fashion, but he'd back the general premise of what Macleod had said. Thank you, God, for people like Jim.

'What are you doing about that?' said the DCI suddenly, desperate to fill the silence that had occurred between the two men.

'Detective Constable Ross is out there now. The rest of my team are sitting, working through profiles, cases, trying to see if we can identify who did this.'

'I think you'll find it's the youths from the estates,' said Simon Mackenzie.

'The trouble with blows like that, sometimes they can be

very disorienting,' said Macleod. 'Probably best for you to give it a day or two before you think about making any serious decisions.'

Simon Mackenzie suddenly took on the red complexion that the DCI had. 'If you don't hunt this person within the next day or two, Macleod, I'm taking this higher up.'

The DCI turned and marched out of the office, got to the door of the outer office, and realised that Simon Mackenzie hadn't followed him. He gave a brief look around, realised he looked stupid, and then marched off out to the hallway, presumably to his own office.

'I get it,' said Simon Mackenzie, 'I really do.'

'With all due respect, Mr Mackenzie, you get what?'

'You. You just want to get on with your job, but we all have a responsibility to stand up.'

'You choose the limelight,' said Macleod. 'You thrive on it; you need to be in it. I need to get to the bottom of cases, and the success I've enjoyed solving some of them has made things difficult for me. For instance, I can't go out there tonight. I'm too well known. As is my colleague, Detective McGrath. Hence, Constable Ross is out there gathering intel for me. I suggest that you let me get on with finding this killer, and I suggest you don't go on to television,' said Macleod, 'and rabbit about these youths. They're not doing it; they're not the killers.'

'What makes you say that? What on God's good earth makes you say that? Have you evidence for that? If so, bring it out to the television. Maybe we'll be able to flush out where this other person is.'

'We don't expose people on television,' said Macleod. 'We don't work that way. We gather our evidence, we arrest, and then it goes to court. Whoever's doing this will see their day in court, and it will be soon. Until then, I suggest you use your influence to calm the situation and not inflame it.'

Mackenzie stared at Macleod, clearly not happy with the response he was getting. He walked out of the door and Macleod made his way over the exit, staring at Simon Mackenzie as he was passing out of the door of the outer office to the hallway beyond. Strictly, the DCI should be accompanying him, but Macleod just wanted him out.

'It was quite a throw though, wasn't it?' It was Clarissa, top of her voice, and it caused Mackenzie to stop for a second before walking on. Macleod looked over at the woman, held up a finger before making his way back inside the office. It was two minutes later when Clarissa put her head in.

'I just wanted to know if the icon is able to accept visitors.'

Macleod looked up, keeping his face as straight as possible. 'You're going to check that attitude,' he said. 'Who is it?'

'Some pretty young thing desperate to sit at the feet of the great Macleod icon, warrior for justice.'

'Shut it,' said Macleod. 'Just shut it,' but she'd done it again, getting underneath him, causing him to react and all he wanted to do was to ignore playing the game and winning.

'It's Kelly McGinley, the social worker. Says she'd like to speak to you. She sounds quite urgent. I told her the icon might not be available.'

'Just let her in,' said Macleod, 'and next time . . . '

Clarissa turned away but Macleod shouted over again, 'Oh, send in Hope. Be useful if she heard this as well.'

Kelly McGinley, dressed in jeans and a pink jumper, walked in, and shook Macleod's hand. She sat down at the conference table and Macleod offered her coffee. He shouted at Hope to get some brought through and he heard her relay the message onto Clarissa. Hope came through, sat down beside Kelly McGinley, and shook hands, and they waited briefly until Clarissa came through with a tray. She placed a cup in front of Hope, one in front of Kelly, and then turned to Macleod. It wasn't his normal cup but it had the words on it, 'MOVIE STAR.' He glared at her.

'One for you, Inspector McQueen. Oh, sorry, Macleod. I forgot—the other one's an icon.' Macleod said nothing but watched Clarissa leave.

'You seem to get on well here,' said Kelly.

'Don't let Sergeant Urquhart cloud your judgment of what a professional force we are. Anyway, I've been watching the riots tonight, Miss McGinley; it's not been good.'

'I was out there,' she said, 'in the early part. Things started to get a bit rough, and I got back off the street. I was trying to calm some of them down, got some of the younger kids to head home. They're not doing this—you do know that?'

'I have my suspicions,' said Macleod, 'but please, what do you know?'

'Well, some of the youth, they seem more agitated. I saw people out there tonight who I don't know. I know you've been bringing people in from other places to help with the riot, but there seems to be people turning up. Now that's bad enough, but some of the kids actually seem put out in their rioting as if other people are taking over.'

'Now that is interesting,' said Macleod. 'I noticed there seems to be a lot more petrol bombings going on. Things seem to be escalating.'

'It's true, and I've never known the kids to be prepared in that way. They pick up rocks, stones because they're lying about.

116

They might go into chairs and that, but we've had looting as well, and don't get me wrong, we've had ones who have gone off joyriding, but it's not about stealing a car—it's about the joyriding. We've had others actually wielding knives to use them. Generally, the knives are not brought out to kill. They're there to discourage others.

'Most of the time on these estates, they were committing antisocial crimes. They were pissed, they were shouting at people, but I heard tonight that one elderly woman was pulled out of her house and her stuff was starting to get stolen. Kids never did that. Don't get me wrong. I'm not defending them for what they have done, but there's an escalation here that's not them. Your constable, Ross, he said that ultimately, they were quite scared, and he's right, they are. What's more is they're now more scared because things are seemingly getting out of hand. They think the other gang is coming over and doing things. They're talking about having to stand up to that, but I looked around and I spoke with my colleague from the other estate. We're seeing lots of people who don't live here.

'That's understood,' said Macleod, 'and thank you for it. I have a little theory going of my own. Go home and stay safe,' said Macleod. 'If you think of anything else, you can let us know. It'll be much appreciated.'

Macleod watched Hope show Kelly McGinley to the door once she'd finished her coffee. When Hope came back in, Macleod was standing looking at the window, contemplating as ever what was going on.

'I think you're right. She thinks you're right. Evidence is starting to point that way. This is a killer on the outside. This is not someone on the estate. This is not the kids.'

'No, it's not,' said Macleod. 'The problem with that is we've got absolutely nothing to go on. I feel like I've just eliminated a whole estate and I still haven't got a clue any more than I did at the start. Who did these acts? We need to start finding out who's ramping this up. Let's hope Ross comes through with something.'

Chapter 14

I t was four in the morning and the riots having calmed down somewhat, Ross placed a call from the old lady's house, asking for some assistance. He didn't give a name but stayed close to the house until he saw the arrival of a couple of uniformed officers to make sure the woman was okay. Shortly afterwards, he saw a medic appear and at that point, Ross took his leave.

The sun was beginning to permeate the sky and the estate wasn't as dark as it had been the previous night. At some point, all the lights had gone out, someone having cut a significant line, but that had been restored sometime after three. Although it was quieter, the police presence was still large.

Ross needed to amble back to his car which was located on the far side of the estate in the garage of a man he had contacted. There was no way Ross was leaving his car in the middle of a riot, but it did mean he had to walk across the entire estate in the early hours of the morning. When he made it back into the station, no doubt Macleod would pressurise him for news about the grenade. Ross thought the grenade was important, but not as important as trying to find out what was happening on the estate, and so he'd made the uncomfortable decision to work through the night.

He'd managed a coffee at the old lady's and she'd been grateful to him, but now he was famished. Continuing his persona of an old drunk, Ross continued to shuffle along, barely looking up at anyone that went past. There were still several young men out and about, the occasional gaggle of girls too, but they were all standing at a distance, away from the officers who had put away their riot gear. They'd be nearby, vans around the corner, but now the key was to calm everything down.

Ross was hobbling across the park area when he saw what looked like a young man handing out money. The kids he was handing it out to could only have been thirteen or fourteen. *What on earth were they doing out at this time of the morning. Was it drugs? Maybe that was at the core of it.* Ross shambled over to where the deal was being done. As he got closer, the man and the youths looked at him once but then ignored him, going back to their dealings. Once whatever transaction was complete, Ross made his way over to the youths.

'What have you got there?' he asked.

'Get off, granddad. Go on, head home.'

'Don't granddad me; what have you got? Anything worth-while?'

'We haven't got anything,' said one of the youths, and Ross looked at the empty hands. He could see there was a fat pocket, however. He quickly reached over, pulled out what was inside. All he could see was money. This was wrong. The exchange went the wrong way. These youths should have been kids picking up the drugs and their money going the other way. He looked at what was rolled up and counted at least five to ten twenties.

'Where the hell did you get that money from?'

'Go on, go away, granddad.'

Ross was shoved by one of the youths and he took a stumble backwards not because he needed it, but because he needed to play his part.

'I said, "Where did you get it?"'

'Look, granddad, we just did a favour for the man there, all right?' The kid turned and pointed to the man who had started to walk away but now he looked back over. He saw Ross and he saw the two kids. Ross stopped pestering the kids, gave a nod, took out his bottle of which he had drunk nearly half the tea, and took another sip. He noted that the man's eyes were still on him.

Ross turned and shuffled away, slowly crossing the park, occasionally sitting down on a bench as if exhausted, but he was looking behind him to see if the man was following. As Ross cleared the park on the far side, possibly a half a mile to his car, he noted that the man was no longer to be seen.

Ross didn't feel like shuffling on, but he had to keep up the persona and walked by a couple of policemen. They asked if he needed any assistance, so he told them to bugger off, growling at them. Then had to issue an apology as they asked what sort of language that was coming from one of the members of the community. Ross spat on the ground and trundled on.

He turned a corner between two large flats and was wandering along when he realised that a car was pulling up just across from him. Someone was getting out with a baseball bat. He only caught the wood emerging from the door with the corner of his eye. Given his current role, he couldn't simply run off but instead turned sharply down the back entrance to one of the set of flats. There were several bins there and Ross

121

made himself small behind a set of them, looking out into the alley as best as he could.

The person with the baseball bat had a hood over their head and he could see eyes peering out. Other than that, they were dressed in camouflage trousers and a dark jacket. Ross thought they looked somewhat like a few of the kids except for one thing. They were bigger and yet certainly not as muscular as some of the older youths.

He crouched down as the figure swept along the alley and started to pull the bins out here and there. Ross was four bins down and he wished now he had climbed into one. He watched as the figure looked around behind him, and then the baseball bat went to the floor and a gun was taken out.

Ross was shaking, but tried to get his brain into gear as to how he would deal with this. There was nowhere to run because he was in an alley. *Could he talk them down? And say what? 'I'm an old man, don't shoot me'? Clearly, they'd been bothered by him talking to the kids and yet he hadn't learned that much.*

Ross crouched down and heard one bin being pulled out and spun across the alleyway. He looked underneath his own cover and could see feet coming closer. He pushed himself back against the wall. Soon they'd be pulling his bin, dragging it from the wall and he'd be left against it. Ross decided he needed to act.

As soon as he felt the bin begin to be pulled, Ross pushed it hard into the figure ahead of him. The figure tumbled, but Ross fought to get around to the bin before the gun holder scrambled to their feet. He put a shoulder down and threw himself at them, knocking them back to the floor and causing the gun to fly across the alley. The gun, however, fired and the bullet ricocheted off the walls, possibly going up higher.

Ross drove a punch down, but found himself suddenly hit in the throat, hard and exact. He tumbled off the figure who scrambled to their feet, and Ross readied himself. After Kirsten Stewart had left, Ross had taken lessons because he always felt he couldn't defend himself as well as his former colleague had. Now he feinted left, caught the figure off guard and threw a right hook that should have floored them, for it caught them right on the chin. As they went to fall, and he went to follow up, he was caught by surprise as the hard punch barely caused a reaction.

Instead, he clocked an uppercut, tumbling backwards. He watched from the ground as the figure strode over towards the gun. Ross looked around desperately, grabbing the baseball bat, and as the figure turned with the gun in hand, Ross launched the bat, catching them clean in the shins, knocking the figure down and the gun dropped again.

Ross could hear cries and shouts from the flats, but the figure once more reached for the gun. Ross desperately thought what else did he have, then pulled the quart bottle of cold tea from his pocket and flung it over, causing it to smash beside the attacker's face. It momentarily lifted them up away from the gun and Ross ran at them, throwing himself as hard as he could.

Together the pair of them smacked into the wall before falling to the floor. The figure was quick, reaching down to choke Ross, but he managed to get two hands on their wrists. They were strong, much stronger than him, although they didn't look like they had muscley arms. He felt the thumbs going into the throat as well, beginning to choke him. Then he heard cries from above.

'What's going on? Get off him. What's that? Get away.'

He saw the figure look around, and then jump to their feet and run off quickly. Ross fought his way up, not needing to pretend he was like an old man for he was desperately trying to get his breath back. He staggered to the end of the alleyway, pushing away a couple of people who asked him if he was all right. By the time he got to the end and looked along the road, the figure was nowhere to be seen. He turned, and announced he dropped his whisky.

'I think it must have smashed,' somebody said.

Ross' concern was not the whisky. Instead, he was more bothered about the gun that was now lying out there. Possibly, they could get some prints from it. Ross staggered back, pushing away those again suggesting he should sit down. As he got close and saw the gun, he turned and sat down so the gun was behind him. As he pretended to puff and pant, he took the gun and stuffed it into the rear of his trousers, letting his jacket fall over the back. He then held an arm out and allowed people to help him up.

'We need to get you a medic, son,' said a man.

'No, I need another bottle. It's all right. Just a fight.'

'They had a gun.'

'No, no, no, no, go home. It's fine,' said Ross. 'It's fine.'

He let his speech drag, but determinedly pushed away from the caring bystanders. He walked off in the opposite direction to his car, but once he'd got around several corners and realised that he was finally alone, he took off the jacket, wrapping the gun up inside and began to sprint, taking a circuitous route round to the car. Once inside, he drove quickly off the estate, realising that police had been called towards the flat. They'd arrived quickly having heard the gunshot, but Ross had been quicker. He picked up his mobile phone in the car and called Macleod, advising him what had happened.

'You need to contact the uniformed boys that have responded. I've got the gun. I'll bring it in for Jona to trace. They can just calm everybody down out there. I didn't want to blow my cover and let it be known we were out and about in case people start getting grabbed thinking they're us.'

'That's good thinking, Alan, but are you okay? I'll send Hope then, pick you up. Go back to your own flat and get a shower. Hope will be with you, then you can come in afterwards. What's the gun like?'

Ross pulled it out from behind him and set it down on the car seat beside him. 'Sir, it looks military to me. Certainly that grade, high powered. It would've blown me away.'

Ross could hear the thoughts of Macleod kicking himself for letting Ross go out and he wanted to tell the inspector that it was okay. But maybe it wasn't; maybe Alan had put himself in a situation he shouldn't have been in. Maybe it was all a little bit too much. He certainly couldn't tell Angus when he got back. He'd talk it over with Hope on the way in.

'Get yourself cleaned up, Ross. Hope will bring you in then afterwards. You've done well. I heard about the little old lady as well.'

'It was weird being out here, sir. Weird. This didn't look like an ordinary riot. There's definitely elements behind this.'

'The person that attacked you.'

'They did it after I talked to some kids, some kids that were paid money,' said Ross. 'Decent money. One hundred, two hundred quid, something like that.'

'What for?' asked Macleod.

'I thought they were looking for drugs. I thought the money

was going the other way. Clearly, somebody's paying them to incite, to cause a riot, fuel it and keep it going.'

'They're willing,' said Macleod, 'to take out anybody that sees that activity. We need to close this down quick. Go get your shower, Ross. I'm afraid I can't let you get back to bed.'

Ross closed the call and continued to drive back towards his flat in the middle of Inverness. He was dog-tired, ready to collapse, but Macleod was right. They needed to get onto this. All that was happening was going to spiral further and further out of control. They needed to get on it before somebody else died.

Chapter 15

Macleod paced around the office, awaiting the arrival of Ross and drew the attention of Clarissa. She'd already marched in with a cup of coffee, but having seen him continue to stalk around his office, she'd walked in without knocking and closed the door behind her.

'If you don't mind, some of us are trying to do some work out there. All we get is this tableau of the running man back and forward, here, there, and everywhere.'

'He got attacked. You got attacked. He was attacked before that. This is not safe now. We need to get this tied up. People have died and more people are going to. You heard about the little old lady last night he saved. I've just got a message through from the Assistant Chief Constable; several in hospital last night. We've got one of our guys with a broken leg. A couple of residents not in very good condition; one critical. Crazy riots, random beatings, and outsiders coming in. We need to get to the bottom of this, close it down quick. It's all over the news again.'

'And you've seen stuff like this before,' said Clarissa. 'You've been in this job as long as I have. Now, admittedly, I never saw somebody burn to death having been nailed to a wall, but outside of that; unrest, tension, come on, Seoras, you're used to that. What's really bugging you?'

He turned away from her to look out of the window.

'That's it. Just go and stare, don't say anything. You're hacked off because you don't know the answer. You don't know even know where to start now.'

'Yes,' he said, 'that's it. That's it exactly. All right? Are you happy?'

'No, I'm not happy, but there's no need for you to be the angry bear; calm down and think. Hope says you've got the best brain in this building. Hope says you work it out. Hope says this and that. Well, if your brain's not working, get hold of the rest of us and use ours.'

'I'm not sure what the head of a person from the art world's going to do.' Macleod was looking out the window as he said it. Clarissa watched him turn a couple of seconds after it came out of his mouth. 'Sorry. Sorry, sorry, sorry. Didn't mean that.'

'Yes, you did. You're missing Kirsten because Kirsten could have run around and handled this business. Kirsten could deal with it because Kirsten's strong. It's not like you and me, get beat up by a couple of these punks, never mind the person that came after Ross. Even Hope's not like that. And you could have bounced off her brain as well. That's what's bugging you, isn't it? That's it.

'I'm not Kirsten, and that's okay, because I'm what you've got at the moment, as is Ross, as is Hope, so quit this angry bear act. Quit this frustration. You want to go and punch a wall, go and punch a wall but you've got a responsibility to this team. You want to get angry, chew out the DCI; the man's a clown anyway, but get on board with this team.'

Clarissa turned and he heard her boots clop across the office.

As she opened the door, he shouted after her.

'Clarissa,' he said, 'thanks.'

'"Damn icon," they said. The least you could do is be like one.'

Macleod was in the wrong and he'd been apologetic, but he thought the least she could have done was give him a smile, not just throw in another dig. Maybe it was ingrained in the woman.

It was five minutes later when Ross walked into the outer office, followed by Hope. She sent Ross off to his desk and made a beeline for Macleod. Macleod had opened the door, but Hope pushed him back inside.

'This was close,' said Hope. 'Told me all about it and this was close. That gun is a serious gun. That's not held by anybody wanting to turn around and say, 'Oh, look at me. I've got a gun, keep out of the way.' That's a gun that gets used. That's a killer.'

'But why?' asked Macleod. 'Is he okay?'

'Alan's not okay. He's coming in, he's going to work at this, but he's not okay.'

'But I need him,' said Macleod. 'I take it the gun's gone to Jona.'

'Yes, I bagged it. Took it in. I took a call as well from the Assistant Chief Constable. He was thanking Ross for picking the gun up and not letting it get out into circulation. It also seems that nobody understood that Ross was out there as an officer. It looks like his cover remained intact.'

'Who would do this?' asked Macleod.

'Well, that's the big question, Seoras, isn't it?' said Hope.

'No, no. It's not a go at you,' said Macleod. 'I mean this, quite simply, who would do it?'

'Let's pull the team in,' said Hope. 'Don't ask this of me and you. You're going to need everybody in on this one. Let's sit and do conference. Not Jona though—she's too busy.'

'Go get them,' said Macleod. 'Get them, sit them down in here. I'll get the coffee.' Macleod made for the door and then realised that Hope was standing, still staring at him. 'What? A man can't get coffee for his colleagues?'

Hope followed him to the door. 'Alan, Clarissa, in here; the boss is getting the coffee.'

There was a shuffling of papers and there was not a single quip from Clarissa as she walked silently to the door. Macleod was aware that there were faces watching him from his office as he stood beside the coffee machine. It needed a fresh dose, so he had to clean out the grains, grind some more up, put them in the filter, and turn the machine on. It was five minutes later when he walked back in with cups for everyone.

'Look,' he said, 'this is probably going to get to us all so right now we need to pull together. I need the three of you with me. I know you are, and I know you're seeing me in a state that I'm not normally in.'

'It's the icon thing, isn't it?' said Clarissa. 'They're charging you with solving with the whole thing and part of you thinks you should. Part of you thinks maybe you are the one. Can I tell you something, Seoras?'

'Okay,' he said.

'You're not. You're the Detective Inspector, and when it comes to murder, you're the best.' Macleod looked up at her. It wasn't like Clarissa that throw out compliments.

'But I have to be honest; poster boy? No, you need to be at the edge, the cutting edge of this, not sounding the bugle. Let that clown upstairs do that. We need your brain on this.'

'Well, I need the rest of yours. Who would do this? Come on. What have we got going on?'

'Well, we've got two estates that are up in arms. We've got two estates, where the cry is that there's gangs running amok,' said Hope.

'But we haven't,' retorted Ross; 'we've got people being paid to set things off.'

'So, who gains?' asked Macleod. 'Who gains from this?'

'Gang Lords?' proffered Hope. 'Maybe there's an agenda there. Maybe it's a territory war. Maybe they're wanting to push up the ante so they can move in afterwards.'

'I don't see it,' said Macleod. 'I don't see it. Before, they were selling their drugs. Business now must be going out the door.'

'And kids are getting paid; the money's not coming the other way,' said Ross.

'Still worth a look though,' said Clarissa. 'Still worth somebody popping out and seeing them, find out what's what. Get their view on it. If it's stopping their business, they'll soon react to that, won't they?'

Macleod nodded. 'If we can't see the answer, maybe we go find someone who needs to know that as well.'

'It's a good idea. Do you want me to go see them then?' asked Clarissa.

'No,' said Macleod, 'Hope goes.' Clarissa looked a little bit annoyed. 'It's nothing against you,' said Macleod, 'it's just a number of these gang lords, well, how do I put this delicately?'

'They don't want their mother coming; they want the Amazonian woman. I get it,' said Clarissa, as she turned to Hope. 'Just to understand that back in my day, I'd have kicked your arse at this.'

Alan Ross blurted out a laugh and then suppressed it. 'Sorry.'

'No, don't be,' said Hope. 'It's good, it's more like the team. So, I'm going to go and look at the gang lords. What about the estate?'

'I have walked that estate. Alan has walked that estate. We have got into trouble and everybody we've spoken to—and that includes uniform speaking to people—we're getting nothing back. People are too scared. We're not going to get our answer from the estate.'

'No, but if we look at who's getting paid.'

'We did,' said Clarissa, 'look what happened to Ross.'

Macleod looked over. Ross tried to smile, but Macleod could see bruising heavy on Ross's neck. The purple and yellow hues would neatly have fitted where thumbs were pressed down.

'Then we'll need to be careful, pairs. Don't walk around on your own. Ross, maybe you can talk to that Kelly McGinley, see if she can tell us anything more. She's got the word on the street.'

'Yes, sir, but I think we need to be careful. She's a civilian; if she starts asking questions like, "Why are you getting paid" and somebody comes at her the way they came after me . . . '

'True,' said Macleod. 'True.' He spun out of his seat and marched over to the window again.

'I thought we were giving that up,' said Clarissa, causing a look from Hope and Ross.

'It's where I stand and think,' said Macleod slowly. 'Talk to her, but not on the estate. When you go into the estate, make sure you go in at least a pair. Make sure you've got your car near you and you can get back out quickly. Go in as the police.'

'I'll tell you now, we'll not get any answers from any of the kids. We could also put them in jeopardy,' said Ross.

'No. No, you won't,' said Macleod. 'I don't think they know

much, but what it will do is tell whoever's doing this that we think it's all coming from the estate, and it's the kids that's doing it. We're going to have to keep them guessing. I can't see us going the correct route. Ross, that handgun, grenade, we need them traced.'

'Will do, sir, might take some time.'

'Then get on it,' said Macleod.

'He's just been up half the night,' said Hope, raising her voice at Macleod.

'Actually, it's been all night,' said Ross, 'but I'm good. I'm good.' He stood up and made for the door, but Macleod spun round.

'Breakfast first. Go down, get yourself a breakfast. Clarissa, go with him. Put it on my account.'

'Account? They actually allow you to have an account? Only people of trust get an account.'

Macleod didn't even smile as Clarissa escorted Ross out of the room; he then turned to Hope. 'I think you're going to be the one. Go and see what they say. Don't be afraid to go down the line if it's good for everybody. Some of these guys, they don't want to get involved in murder, especially when it's not them; it's not a rival. If things are bad for business, they'll also want to react at some point. We can't have that. Go see what you can find out.'

As Hope went to leave, Macleod's phone rang and he picked it up.

'Detective Inspector Macleod,' he almost regretted saying it as he realised the number was home.

'Well, you're sounding formal. I've got your shirts, love. I'm going to drop them down later today if that's okay. I know you don't like me about when you're in the middle of something like this.'

'Hope's going to be up close to that way,' said Macleod. 'I'm sure she wouldn't mind picking them up.' He put his hand up indicating Hope should stay in the room and she stepped back from the door. 'You don't mind picking up a couple of my shirts, bringing them in?'

'No,' said Hope, 'that's fine,' but clearly, she was a little bit agitated. There was plenty going on.

Maybe she wondered why Jane couldn't bring them in, thought Macleod. 'I'd get them myself, but I'm not going to see home and they're asking for me up above. You'll be out that way, Hope; okay?'

Hope nodded. 'Okay. Tell her I'll be there after I go off and see this gang lord.'

Macleod turned back to the phone. 'Hope's going to pick them up, love, okay? She's just got a bit of work out that way and then she'll pick them up. What else are you doing today?'

Macleod didn't even hear the answer, his mind elsewhere, thinking about the estate. 'Love you,' he finished with, aware that he hadn't a clue what Jane had spoken about. As Hope closed the door, Macleod could feel himself clench his fist. The answer must be out there. He just couldn't see it.

Chapter 16

Hope McGrath had recovered her leather jacket from Ross and zipped it up as she stepped out of the car. They were on the outskirts of Inverness, not far from the estates where all the trouble had been kicking off, but in a very different place. Here, five-bedroom houses were the norm and the particular one she was standing in front of now could well have had more.

It had two pillars at the front of the house and a driveway that swept in front. Behind it, she could see a summer house and even a pool somewhere in the middle of a green expanse. The person she was here to see, known as Burnsey or Johnny Burns, was a local gang lord, well known for running drugs, but hard to nail down on anything. The drug division of the local force had plenty of information on him. And while they'd picked up many who worked in his service, they couldn't get anything tangible to link back to Burns.

As Hope approached the house, two men stepped out of the front door, both as tall as her and significantly wider. She reached inside her jacket and took out her warrant card.

'I'm Detective Sergeant Hope McGrath. I was hoping to have a word with Mr Burns if he's in.'

One of the large men gave a rap on the door behind him. It

opened and a smaller figure stuck his head out. 'She says it's Sergeant McGrath for Mr Burns.'

The smaller man looked up at Hope. He had black hair, but it was greased back, giving the attitude of a weasel. 'And what can Mr Burns do for you?'

'That would be between Mr Burns and myself. He's probably very aware that there's some disturbing incidents going on. Let's say I could use his help.'

'And what if Mr Burns doesn't want to help?'

'Then Mr Burns can tell me that himself. As for you, kindly get inside that house and tell Mr Burns I am here. I'd rather not go and get my boss to haul Mr Burns down to the station. At the moment, I'm here as a friendly call; nothing more, nothing less.'

The man stared for a moment then disappeared back inside the door. Hope went to follow, but the two larger gentlemen stepped across.

'Not being funny, love,' said one of them, 'but nobody goes in until Mr Burns says so.'

'Let's hope Mr Burns does say so then,' said Hope. 'I'd hate to have to bring Mr Burns out.'

The two men looked at each other for a moment, clearly sizing up Hope, whether or not she was capable of doing that on her own. Two minutes later, the door behind the two men opened and they stepped aside. The weasel was back.

'Mr Burns will see you now. Kindly follow me.'

Hope let the man lead her through a marble-floored hallway, past a well-fitted kitchen and out to a summer room at the rear of the house. Beyond it, Hope could see a man sitting on a large chair, watching someone swimming in a pool beyond. As she walked through the summer house and round to Burns, she was introduced by the weasel who then scurried out of the way.

'My apologies for disturbing you,' said Hope. 'Detective Sergeant Hope McGrath. I was hoping to have a little discussion with you.'

'Well, well, if it isn't Hope McGrath; seen you on the telly, love. You look a lot better than that other one—surprised he's not here himself.'

'He felt you may respond better to me,' said Hope. The man offered Hope a seat across from him with an open hand. She unzipped her leather jacket, taking it off and putting it over the back of the chair, before sitting upright in her crisp blue t-shirt.

'He's not wrong there,' said Johnny Burns, 'but I don't flatter easily.'

'Good,' said Hope, and cast her eyes over the man. He was smaller than she was. His hair was balding. He looked to be at least mid-fifties if not older. The sound of laughter from the pool made her turn her head. She was expecting to see some young plaything of the man, but instead, a middle-aged woman was throwing two kids around in the pool. She was dressed modestly in a swimsuit and Hope motioned to them.

'Are we okay to talk in front of—'

'At the moment,' said Johnny, 'I assume this is going to be a pleasant conversation. Obviously, if there was anything you wouldn't want brought up in front of my children and their nanny, then you won't do it and you'll ask to go inside.'

'Okay,' said Hope, 'I can work with that. I take it you've been looking at the news recently?'

'I wondered when you'd be here. Yes, it's disturbing, isn't it? Knockmalley estate and the Walmsley. Wondering if it would spill over onto a few others.'

'To be candid,' said Hope, 'you carry out an awful lot of business on those estates. How are you feeling about the current issues?'

The man reached forward to a decanter that was sitting on a low table in front of the seat. He took a whisky tumbler and poured himself an inch or two of it before offering to Hope.

'I'm on duty,' she said. 'Not something I can do.'

'A little orange juice then?' he said. 'Cup of tea, coffee? We have some good stuff here.'

'Well, if you're feeling generous, I'll take a coffee.'

Johnny Burns clicked his fingers and the weasel-like man appeared and was sent scurrying for coffee. Johnny then sat back, the whisky in his hand. He sipped on it, looking thoughtful.

'It's not good for business, it really isn't. Now I know that probably would make you glad in normal circumstances, but you wouldn't be here if there wasn't a catch to what was going on.'

'What do you mean?' asked Hope and then smiled as the weasel-like man appeared with a coffee, placing it in front of her and then backing away.

'Well, you're murder squad; yourself and Macleod, you'll have been called in because of the deaths of these young people, but with the riot and that's going on, one would think you'd be all over that estate pulling people in. You've pulled nobody in so far. It'll be a closed shop, of course. I could go in and try and say a few words to people, but it's not my style. I don't mess with anyone who's not messing with my business.

'However, lately things seem to be difficult business-wise, hard to sell. This is due to the rather fractious nature of what's going on. I'd prefer a return to calmer times, and to be honest with you, I have thought about whether or not I need to step in. The difficulty is that it's not easy to take a heavy hand when you've got the likes of your boss stepping into the fray.'

'I'm sure he'd be delighted to hear it, so I take it you haven't had any involvement so far?'

'None,' said Johnny. 'Absolutely none. When you get chaos like this, some people then big themselves up, think they are more than they are. I'm surprised you're even here asking.'

'I wouldn't be, except that there's a lot of money changing hands out there.'

Johnny looked up from his whisky. 'Really?'

'One of our guys was out there. What disturbed him was he thought he saw someone selling product to children; well, youths. Turned out they were giving the kids money.'

'Well, that I don't do. You see, I'm sure you know how it works. If you're a seller, you want people to be giving you the money.'

'And that's what put us onto it. But we also thought someone like yourself prefers to operate in an environment that's protected. You like a reasonable semblance of order. Somebody's coming in and paying other people to make it not so, but we're also getting calls for a task force to go in and sort the estates out. That would affect you greatly as well. The boss is worried that if it isn't you doing this, you're going to react soon.'

'Your boss is an astute man, although I can't say that I'm a particularly big fan of his. However, you can tell him from me that I don't intend to get involved unless things get out of hand, and it's not me in the first place. The first guy that died, Peter Olive . . . '

Hope was impressed that the man knew the name.

'Peter Olive was a little punk, went around beating up on the younger ones but he didn't do anything to me. I had no reason to do it. And from what I heard, stabbed lots of times. Stabbed with an item that doesn't really go with the estate.'

'You heard well,' said Hope. 'I won't ask where you got that from. Not really what one of your guys would use though, is it?'

Johnny nodded at the kids in the pool. 'Let's be a bit more discreet than that. But, no, my employees would not resort to such items. They certainly would be smaller. The problem is, Miss McGrath, or should I say Hope?'

'The coffee's good enough for you to say what you want. Guess you will anyway.'

'Always good to be polite to a lady,' he said. 'No, well, the point is, that a lot of the dealers are starting to get scared. A lot of the youths are getting hysterical, whipped up. A few of my dealers have had things said to them. One's been threatened, product taken without payment. It's not good for business; it's not good for me.

'Sometimes it's good to have a reputation. The trouble with a reputation is, and I say this from an entirely business perspective, you must maintain that reputation when it's challenged. There's too many challenging, too many young ones whipped up—they're foolish. They don't understand who they're going up against or why. So, so far, I've not got involved. If it continues, yes, I'll be involved. Or at least certain associates will make things known.'

'It would be appreciated by Inspector Macleod if you could hold off for a while; let us try and haul in whoever this individual is.'

'I would say that the individual is pretty well-practiced. Grenade tossed into a car, as for Jai Smith, put up against a wall, held there, paraffin chucked over, set alight. What would you have to do to be worthy of that sort of treatment? How would you have ever offended someone?'

'Okay,' said Hope, 'so it's not you.'

'No, it's not. And like I said, I'm refraining from doing anything because your man is on the case and he's like a bloodhound. These other killings, they're not me. That's why I'm just chilling out for a few days with the kids.'

'Where's Mrs Burns then?'

'Just chilling out somewhere, taking her time. I said I'd keep an eye on the kids for a while. Keeps me out of trouble. You ever thought about kids yourself? You look like you could make a man a good wife.'

Hope stood up, took her coffee, turned to look at the kids and drank. As she looked at the kids, she thought that was a part of her life that might pass by, one she wasn't interested in, but now she had met John, her care-hire manager turned lover, she was looking at certain previous certainties thinking she may have to re-evaluate them.

Johnny Burns stood up, put his hand out. 'It's been good talking with you, Detective Sergeant. Tell your boss I'm glad you came for the chat, didn't just storm in. I know he doesn't like my kind and quite frankly, I probably don't really like his. But there's no need for things to get sour when we haven't got anything to do with it.

'However, I will react if I need to. Tell him to find these people quick. And as for you, Miss McGrath, give my best wishes to your car-hire man.'

Hope felt a chill run down her spine. Of course, somebody

141

like this would know who she was attached to. He'd done it very pleasantly, leaving it to the last moment to indicate that this entire conversation was not going anywhere else.

'You have my confidence in this,' said Hope. 'Thank you for your cooperation. It's appreciated.'

'And that gun,' said Burns, as Hope walked away, 'didn't come from any stock of mine. I think that's military grade. I'm not sure how you could get hands on that one.'

Hope nodded her thanks and turned to walk out to the front doors. As she approached them, the two large men opened them for her and gave a nod.

'Be seeing you,' she said over her shoulder, and she could hear the slight consternation she had caused. *Well, that was one off the list*, she thought. *We can tick that off.* It was time to head over to Macleod's and pick up his shirts from Jane.

Chapter 17

Hope turned off the A9 onto the back road that led through the Black Isle. Macleod's house was located close to the Moray Firth and had a view overlooking it, but to get there, you had to go through some back roads and find a house that was set into trees. Hope stopped to let someone pass by, the track being so narrow that only one car could get through, but she was in a relatively good mood as she approached Macleod's residence.

Johnny Burns had been good; he'd said what was happening. He seemed to be holding back, giving them a chance to sort out what was happening on the estate before he might take matters into his own hands. His reputation was fearsome despite the rather idyllic scene that Hope had found him in. Maybe next time she'd be speaking to him in a more formal nature. She hoped not.

As Hope turned the corner that led along towards Macleod's house, she saw several cars parked up. There was yelling in the air, a noisy crowd of what looked like youths, possibly teenagers and above, all chanting and yelling. Hope didn't like the look of it and immediately picked up the phone calling the police station, asking them for backup. Whatever the reason, it wasn't going to be a good one; after all, this was Macleod's house.

While he didn't exactly live in an incognito fashion, it was unusual to find this number of people at his abode. Also, they were not sitting chanting and supporting him, instead, they seemed to be arguing, not just with each other but with somebody from the house. Hope immediately thought of Jane, stepped out of the car, and started striding towards the largest number of youths.

'It's the redhead,' somebody shouted and Hope started telling them to move back. Several of them moved to block her path and she glanced over at the house noting that the door had been kicked in. A neighbour was there telling people to go back but they were being shouted down by the other youths. *They must be thirty to forty here*, thought Hope. *If they come at me, I haven't got a chance*.

'What's going on?' she asked. 'What the heck's this?'

'We got Macleod's woman,' said one youth, dancing, holding up a beer can while he was doing it. 'They're in there giving her what for.'

Hope took one look at him, then bolted towards the door. A burly bloke stood in front of her.

'Get out of my way,' said Hope, 'or God help me, I'll make sure that face never sees the sun again.'

She took the man by surprise but as he stepped back several of the others egged him to take her in hand, show her who the boss was. As he reached for her, Hope jabbed straight fingers into his throat causing him to choke and double up. She casually knocked him aside. Others began to close around her. She started to run, saw one stretch his leg out to trip her up, jumped, and came down on it with a sickening crack. Hope wasn't shabby when she moved, and she tore off to the front door where the neighbour was fighting a losing battle to keep others out. Hope grabbed the nearest to him, spinning around and throwing him back into the crowd of her pursuing foes.

There was a moment when they seemed to fall over each other, giving a momentary break in the pursuit during which Hope grabbed the neighbour and pulled him inside. She thought about shutting the door, but she couldn't. Hope tore up the stairs looking to see if Jane was in the bedroom after the comments had been made from out the front. As she tore around, there was no one there.

Then she heard a cry from the neighbour down below. Hope exited the bedroom, but not before picking up a large statuette. She could see several thugs coming up the stairs now. She ran down, swinging the statuette in front of her, catching one man on the chin. He fell backwards and she kicked hard, helping him tumble down into the others. She put two hands on the banister, threw herself over and landed in the hallway. Beyond her, out by the kitchen, was the neighbour tussling with one foe but shouting at Hope that Jane was outside.

Hope raced through to the kitchen, grabbed the punk off the man and flung him, watching as his head bounced off one of the cupboards. Hope ran out onto the patio to find Jane in a half-stripped state. The blouse she was wearing was ripped, and she was standing in her bra and her underwear, tights up around her hips. In front of her several youths danced, pants down around their ankles waving their manhood at her. Hope raced forward, grabbed one of them and flung him. He tripped up stumbling into the others in a semi-naked pile.

Hope threw punches left and right and struck into throats causing them to choke. 'Here,' she said and took Jane's hand.

The woman desperately grabbed hold of her and Hope took her in hand.

Seeing Jane's face a mess of tears, she didn't stop to ask what had happened to her but instead started dragging her back towards the house. Her options were the car but that was on the other side of everyone, or she could flee down to the Moray Firth, down into the undergrowth, or she could get to the safe room.

Previously, Jane had been attacked in their own home but this was by a killer who intended to put her into an acid bath. Hope had come to the rescue on that day but had paid for it with an acid scar across her face. Since that day, Jane had never been entirely comfortable and so Macleod had installed a safe room, somewhere to go and hide if something happened. Not many people knew about it but he had mentioned it to Hope who had said it was a good idea, but he hadn't said where it was. She grabbed Jane.

'Where's the safe room? Where is it?'

'Out by the wood, the shed,' she said.

'The shed?'

Hope looked up. Coming through the house was the horde, and to the side of the house there were more coming round, but beyond them she saw the small shed. She thought it had simply been Macleod's new place to put the lawnmower but apparently not. It seemed this is where his bunker was, where his safe room had been installed.

Rather than run straight for it and into a crowd of possibly ten to fifteen youths, Hope turned and dragged Jane to the front of the patio, stepping over it and running down into the bush below. It was steep and Jane was in her bare feet, shouting every time she stood on something. The poor woman was still

146

in her tights and nothing to cover her modesty on top, except her underwear.

The neighbour had followed. A man somewhat older than Hope and while clearly, he'd been enthusiastic in trying to help, he certainly wasn't up for the fight. She saw blood running from his nose already.

Hope edged around the side of the hill that led down to the Moray Firth and thought about going lower and lower. She could call, ask for the coastguard to launch. They could probably get the lifeboat in and she could enter the water and go for it. Was Jane a good swimmer? She didn't know. By the time they called them and got scrambled, it could be too late.

She looked up and saw the horde scrambling down. Hope decided to circle, run around the side of the hill and she pulled Jane on. She got through a group of trees that were in a line down the hill, shielding off others from behind from seeing them. Immediately she pointed to Jane and to the neighbour, telling them to climb up as fast as they could.

She stopped to look around, picked up a branch from a tree. It was thick in her hands, and she thought at least, it wouldn't break. She stopped and held her ground as the first man ran through, he was caught under the chin and lifted off his feet. Two more followed him, suddenly trying to backpedal as Hope thrashed them both with the branch.

Another came through ducking under her attack, throwing his shoulder into her, knocking her off her feet. She rolled desperately, knowing she had to get up. She had that fear, seeing what they'd started doing to Jane. If they couldn't have had their fun with her, would they come for Hope?

She managed to roll off her assailant who grabbed her boot only to find the other one planted into his face. Hope stood up, grabbing the stick and clobbered another one across the head as he came through. She then turned and started running as hard as she could up the hill.

It was Hope's gamble that everyone would come down after them. After all, that was the point, wasn't it? They'd come for Jane. Come for Macleod's woman. There had to be sirens arriving soon, but Hope knew that the Black Isle was a good fifteen minutes outside of Inverness at best. They'd have to scramble across the bridge.

Maybe they were lucky and got one or two units close, but they were going to need a whole hoard to deal with this, possibly scrambling those who were already up from Glasgow and Edinburgh to cover the riots at night.

This was one time in her life when she wished she was armed, to hold them back with some shots. Of course, Macleod would never have a gun on the premises. He abhorred them. 'Wouldn't want to use one' is what he said if the situation got out of control.

Hope looked back down the hill and the hoard were now scrambling up behind her. How out of control did he want it to be?

Hope broke through, up onto the driveway to see Jane and the neighbour being accosted by six different youths. Some of them seemed younger, but there was an older man orchestrating them and it was to him that Hope ran. She ignored what some of the younger ones were doing to Jane, instead, approaching the man, and going straight with her fist towards his face. He tried to duck, but she connected the back of his head with one punch and hit him with another two. Her knuckles were starting to bleed. Whenever you trained with the bags, you did it with gloves on. She wasn't used to this

148

much violence.

Some of the younger boys who were pulling at Jane seemed disturbed by the man being attacked and the neighbour managed to throw one off. Hope grabbed another, unconcerned for his safety as she flung him spiralling into a tree; he fell to the ground, his nose bloodied.

Hope turned to see the rest. Jane managed to slap one across the face, and she'd scratched with her nails causing streaks of blood to appear across his cheek. Hope grabbed the woman, yelling at the neighbour to follow, and went directly for the shed. She looked to see there was no lock on it, pulled it open and saw inside. There was a metal door on the floor. She reached for it, pulling it up and saw steps leading down. Her eye caught a set of garden shears on the wall.

She turned yelling at Jane to get down into the bunker and looked for the neighbour, but he had been caught by several of the youths on his way over. The man was kicked and punched, and Hope ran out, the garden shears in hand, swinging them indiscriminately. She caught the shoulder of one man who screamed then spun around again, catching another across the chest. With a few more blows she managed to break the neighbour free and ran for the bunker, letting the door close after them, and watched Jane initiating the locking process.

Emergency lights came on and Hope took some deep breaths. Jane sat down on the floor, crying, but Hope looked over at the neighbour who had a large gash running down his side. She looked and saw a knife wound, placing two hands on it.

'Is there a phone?' asked Hope.

'No phone, we've closed the doors, the signal's gone. They'll come,' said Jane. 'They'll come. Dear God, they have to come.'

Above them, they could hear a hoard fighting away at doors

that were refusing to budge. Hope would've been happy, calm almost, except for the wound to this neighbour, for the man was struggling to stay with her.

'Who is this?' said Hope.

'Mr Almond; he lives next door,' said Jane.

'Mr Almond,' said Hope, 'you stay with me. It's going to be okay. You stay with me.' Almond's eyes flicked open, but they were swimming. 'Have we got anything down here?' asked Hope, 'Anything, any bandages? Anything to keep the bleeding—'

'No, nothing. It's just a safe room. There's nothing in here. It's just . . . '

Hope nodded, keeping her hands down, 'Don't talk to me, talk to him. Talk to him, ask him about his house. Whatever. Just keep him talking. Keep him talking.'

Above the clamour of people trying to break in above, Hope could hear sirens. *They've got to be here soon*, she thought; *they've got to be here soon.*

It sounded like a riot above and then it got worse, people charging in and out of the shed. It was another twenty minutes before there was a solid repetitive tap.

'Are you there? Are you there?'

'We're here, Seoras. I need an ambulance now. I need an ambulance. Jane, open the door, open the door.' Jane was sitting on her backside, still breathing heavily, shaking. 'The number, Jane,' said Hope, 'please. Open the door. Mr Almond needs it.'

It took Jane another thirty seconds to compose herself, press the buttons, and Macleod raced first down the steps. He saw Hope and shouted at some paramedics to help her before flinging his arms around Jane and holding her tight.

150

Hope walked up the steps five minutes later, after the paramedics had taken away Mr Almond. She'd seen a faint smile from the man, which was some comfort, but as she reached the top, she looked down at her hands, seeing the blood drip off them. She looked around up Macleod's lawn, large divots torn up, bits and pieces smashed. The house had several windows knocked in. Who knew what the house looked like inside? From behind her, she saw Jane in a blanket being led away with Macleod.

'What do you want me to do, Seoras?' she asked.

'Get them. Find out who did this.'

She watched him disappear into the back of an ambulance. His face was thunderous. She looked across as a new car arrived, small and green, with a woman in a shawl in the front and a man sitting beside her with a neat suit on.

Thank God, thought Hope. *Thank God. They're here.*

Chapter 18

Macleod strode into the outer office and noticed his team stand up as he did so. He wasn't in the mood for talking so he marched straight towards his door, opened it, and saw there was already someone inside his office.

'Jim,' he said, 'what's up?'

'How is she, Seoras? Is she okay?'

'She's traumatized,' Macleod told the Assistant Chief Constable, 'but she's not physically harmed.'

'Hope saved her.'

'Well, I don't want to think about it if Hope hadn't been there. My neighbour's pretty shook up as well. God love the guy; he's of an age when he shouldn't be doing things like that.'

'Indeed,' said Jim. 'We got there as soon as we could.'

'I'm thankful for it. Tell all the boys and girls, really. The house is a mess, though.'

'I've left a couple of them up there just to keep an eye on it. Obviously, you'll need to let me know how you want to go about putting it back together. Have you got somewhere to stay in the meantime? Book a hotel if you need it. On us; put Jane in there if you want as well.

'She's up at the hospital at the moment,' said Macleod. 'They said they're going to keep her in overnight for observation—probably best for her. Get a little rest.'

'Well, is there anything I can do for you?'

Macleod nodded. Jim was one of the good guys, competent in his own job but Macleod could tell something was up.

'What's up?' asked Macleod. 'There's something you want to say, and you don't look like you want to say it.'

'Well, you're going to get a visit in a minute. I tried to ward him off, the DCI. I can overrule him and I told him to back off, but the Chief Constable's been sold the idea. Looks like your DCI was all over him. I'm sorry. I can't do anything. I've said my part but they're not listening.'

'Not this campaign, not this being a poster boy. Not right now. I've got enough on my plate.' Macleod realised that his voice was extremely raised and looking out through the interior windows of his office, he saw his staff looking over, concerned.

'Exactly what I said, Seoras, and I told her that in no uncertain terms, but the Chief Constable actually thinks having your face up there is going to do some good. Don't ask me how they sold it to her. I can't stay. I've got to get back because with you being a poster boy, I've got to get these neighbourhoods quiet.'

'Well, thanks, Jim,' said Macleod. 'Thanks for letting me know.'

'Tell Jane I was asking for her. Keep her safe and anything you need, remember, just say.' Macleod lifted his hand as Jim left the office. Within ten seconds, the door to his office had opened again with Hope looking in.

'How're you doing?'

153

'How do you think I'm doing?' said Macleod. 'She's just . . . this is worse than last time, Hope. Last time she was shook up, I put the safe room in, and she . . . well, thought she was safe.'

'Safe from what, though?' said Hope.

'You did it though,' said Macleod. 'It's the second time you've come to her rescue. It's not right. She got all of this because of me. Both times it was because of me. The first time that killer was coming after me, after all my cases, what I had done, people knew. This time. Well, this time . . .'

'This time they came for you, too,' said Hope. 'They went after you in a way that was smart. Look at you. Agitated, wound up, not in control.'

'What do you expect?'

'Not suggesting you're doing anything wrong. I'm just saying they came for you. If they come at you head-on, they won't knock you off. They can't. You're a stubborn son of a bitch and you'll just go right back at them.'

Macleod lifted his eyes to Hope, almost warning her off.

'Well, it's true. You are. You put that head down, you run at things. I know that you drive this team when it comes to it, but they went for your soft spot. Why? What are they wanting from it?'

There was a knock at the door, and it opened to reveal the face of the DCI. Macleod was not prone to swearing but he thought this time, he might have to control his own tongue.

'Detective Chief Inspector,' said Macleod. 'Oh look, Mr Mackenzie as well behind the DCI.'

Simon Mackenzie stepped in, offering a hand forward. 'Let me be the first to say how sorry I was hearing about your dear wife. How is she?'

'She's in hospital. She's not good.'

154

'That is why you need to be coming onto this campaign. You need to be at the front of this operation. We need you now, Macleod.'

As a senior officer, Macleod should have at least offered him a seat, talked to him one-to-one, honestly and openly, but with respect. Instead, Macleod turned away and walked over to the window. It was only as he turned, he realised there was someone out in the office beyond.

'Is there somebody else out there?' asked Hope.

'Just my wife,' said Simon Mackenzie.

'Well, bring her in,' said Hope. 'Don't leave her standing there.'

Hope marched over to the door and called the woman through. She had short, black hair cut into a small bob and wore a baggy jumper with some jeans. Clearly, she hadn't been intending to come in because she didn't look like she was dressed to impress. However, she smiled all round.

'I'm sorry for your wife, Detective Inspector.'

'Let me introduce my wife,' said Simon Mackenzie. 'Alice is my better half and I mean that in so many ways. You always need a good, strong woman behind you. I feel about her probably how you feel about Jane, Detective Inspector.'

Macleod didn't turn around. *How did he know how he felt about Jane?*

'You'll have to excuse the Inspector,' said Hope. 'It's all been quite a shock.'

'And you raced to the rescue?' said the DCI. 'Fantastic. I can see the pair of you up there.'

'Up there,' said Hope. 'No. We've got stuff to do here. We need to get on with it.'

'Don't you see?' said Simon Mackenzie. 'Now is the time;

155

things have gone, beyond a limit, we need a rallying figure—a figure the public knows. We need Macleod out there, the one the public trust. And beside him, like an avenging angel, yourself, Sergeant McGrath; even the mark on your face makes you look like someone who can handle herself, handle the street.'

Hope inadvertently raised a hand up and touched her scar. It was a wound that had certainly disfigured her to some degree. At best, she tried to not make it the main feature of her face. She realised that many people were caught out by it. Amongst the team, no one noticed. Elsewhere it had caused people to stare. She remembered one man's comment of 'It's a rough picture; pity when you look at the body that goes with it.' It took all her strength and restraint not to put that punk through the wall. If Clarissa had been with her, it was doubtful the man would have survived.

'I don't think that's a good idea,' said Hope. 'We've got a murderer out there and we have to get on top of this case. That's how we do it; that's how we stop all this. We go down our line of finding who did it and we bring them to justice; then everyone can see who it is.'

'Isn't it these kids running around? Simon's always on about them. They said a lot of the locals are fed up with it and now we've got the rioting on; it's just not on.'

Macleod listened to the voice of Alice Mackenzie and something on the back of his neck made the hairs rise. Simon Mackenzie was street smart. He spoke well, he was a counsellor, a politician. He knew how to work things. His wife, however, was coming across as a bit of a klutz. Macleod wasn't sure he bought it.

'Well, I'm afraid the point's moot,' said the DCI. 'The Chief

Constable has asked for this.'

'With all due respect to the Chief Constable,' said Hope, 'this is extraneous. This is not the normal duty and not what we signed up for. I am not going to have my mug paraded around just because you think I look like some sort of attractive Valkyrie on the shoulder of my friend.'

Friend, thought Macleod. *Yes, she is, and she's defending me to the hilt.*

'Well, the point is moot. Macleod, come and see me in twenty minutes. I'll give you a briefing about how this is going to go.'

Macleod spun on his heel and slammed his fist onto his desk. There began an eerie silence as he said nothing, but looked up into the gaping stares of the DCI and Simon Mackenzie.

'No, don't you try and force me. I'll take a leave of absence. I will walk out that door and I've got every reason to. I've got a partner who's just been attacked. The mental trauma I'm in, I could walk out of here for three to four months. So far, I've had two of my team attacked; I've had my own partner attacked. I am heavily invested in this case. I will bring your murderer to justice, I will bring them kicking and screaming,' said Macleod. His calm but deliberate tone was incredibly unsettling. 'They will go through the courts for what they have done. Now, with all due respect, get out of my office.' Macleod turned and looked out the window again.

There was a brief silence and then Macleod heard feet shuffling away before the door closed. He turned round hoping to find an empty office, but McGrath stood the opposite side of the desk.

'I hope your pension's good,' said Hope. 'That was altogether a bit of a . . . '

'Don't. I meant every word. I meant every single word. I'm

not having this. I'm not.'

'Calm down, Seoras,' said Hope. 'Calm down, I got to her; she's safe. I got to her.'

'She's not safe; she's trembling like a leaf. I barely got away. They had to give her some sleeping tablets so she could get some rest. It's not okay.'

'No, it's not,' said Hope, 'but she's alive and she's safe. I got her.'

Macleod walked round the desk to Hope and put two hands up, one on either cheek. He looked into her face and gently pulled her head forward to give her a kiss on the forehead.

'I thank you; you did,' he said. 'God alone knows how much I do.'

'I got it, Seoras. Time to work; time to work.'

There was a rap at the door and Macleod glanced past McGrath to see Ross. He waved him in.

'Just wanted to come in and say how sorry I was, sir. How is she doing?'

'She's not great,' said Hope. 'She's physically okay but it's taken a toll on her.'

'Well, I'm sorry about that.'

'We need to get back out there,' said Macleod. 'I need you back out on the street, Ross. I need you to get me something. They're trying to put me on this task force to go in and I've refused it, so we better come up with our murderer. I just can't see who.'

'May I?' asked Ross. Macleod looked and Ross was pointing to the conference table.

'Of course, I'll just call Clarissa in.'

Two minutes later, the four of them were sat down at the conference table where Ross was leaning forward, two elbows on the desk as if he were thinking hard.

'This probably shouldn't go outside this room but think about what's happened.'

'You mean the riots?' asked Hope.

'The riots, everything. We get three murders none of which quite fit the bill to be a random killing. We've got a grenade involved; we've got a knife being used in an incredibly brutal way. Now, to the public these all look like they've been done by people on the estate, but not to us. We're not that daft. We don't have an individual putting somebody up against the wall and setting light to them. From what we know, it's a random individual they picked. So why? Could have been anyone as long as the youths suffer.'

Macleod sat back and Hope thought she could see his eyes coming back into focus. *The brain's starting to tick*, she thought.

'They want a task force. Who does the task force benefit?' asked Ross.

'The estates, calms them down,' said Clarissa.

'No,' said Macleod. 'Yes but no, you're right. That's the purpose of it or the stated purpose of it but Ross is right. Who does it benefit?'

'The DCI; he's heavily involved in it.'

'The DCI may not be my man of choice but he's no murderer,' said Macleod. 'He's one of us—not always the most intelligent of us, but he's one of us.'

'The other person at the front of it is Simon Mackenzie,' said Ross. 'Simon Mackenzie has come back time and again. The amount of times you've turned him down, most people would've turned around and said, 'Right, let's find someone else because, with all due respect, you're not the only face here. You're not the only one that can front the campaign.'

Ross's face was almost apologetic, but Macleod nodded.

'He is right, and they went for your soft spot,' said Hope.

'We've been attacked out doing the job,' said Ross, 'but that's bread and butter. Did he think that if I got a knife in the gut that you'd jump on the task force? If so, it's clearly somebody that doesn't know you.'

'Keep running with it,' said Macleod.

'They went for Jane because it would unbalance you. It would make you upset, or so they thought.'

'You were unbalanced,' said Hope. 'You really were.'

'I still am,' said Macleod. 'I still am. Although I just chewed them out and threw them out of the room, there was part of me that given time might have come round to it because we weren't getting anywhere. We weren't finding anything.'

'Let me investigate Simon Mackenzie,' said Ross. 'Let me do the works on him. I think that's where it's coming from. I think there's a tag in here and because it's me, they won't see it coming. If you start asking questions or Hope does, they'll be all over it.'

'Clarissa here's got the subtlety of a brick,' said Macleod. Clarissa looked up, gave him a grin and a feint that she was offended, before nodding.

'Alan's your man,' she said.

'Go then, Ross,' said Macleod, 'look at Mackenzie but we need cover. Clarissa, keep on the street. See if you can trace where that money has come from. Talk to some of the younger people because even if it is Mackenzie, there's other things going on behind this; he can't be everywhere at once.'

'There's also another problem,' said Hope.

'Yes, his height. He's not that far shorter than you,' said Macleod. Jona said that the arms weren't stretched far apart with Jai Smith because the person that did it was smaller.'

'I never said he did the killing,' said Ross. 'I just said he was a driving force, someone behind it.'

'Go check him out,' said Macleod, 'but be careful. Everyone, be careful.'

Chapter 19

R oss put his arms up in the air, stretched out, and felt the ache in his limbs. Over the last few days, he didn't want to know how little sleep he had. A call from Angus earlier on the day was comforting, but he'd had to tell him that he probably wouldn't see him at the house due to the ongoing situation.

Ross thought himself fortunate that his partner was at least understanding. When he'd heard about Jane's situation, Angus had offered to go down to the hospital and sit with her. Ross had thought it a good idea, that Jane would be able to speak to someone who at least partly understood what she was going through. Everyone else who had visited would probably be from the force or a neighbour, but Angus had the same perspective as Jane. It wasn't that long ago that Angus had his own situation to deal with.[1]

The screen in front of Ross had certain manifests that the military had spoken to him about, showing the grenade's movement amongst various stations. However, there was no record of loss. Ross had spent several hours chasing his own

---

[1]   See Kirsten Stewart Thrillers #7: The Man Everyone wanted

tail, trying to find out where you could get a grenade and a handgun, and so far, worked out that if they'd come from the military depots, the military didn't know about them being missing.

In fairness, they'd been very cooperative, and he was asking awkward questions, but they too had seen the pictures on TV. It's quite possible the military were going to be brought in soon to start patrolling the streets, and it was a prospect that neither they, nor the police force, particularly enjoyed.

On Ross's other screen, a profile of Simon Mackenzie had highlights running through it. As Ross was stretching, he saw Jona march into Macleod's office. She held a small brown file under her arm, which usually meant she'd brought stuff over from forensics for Macleod to look at. Thirty seconds later, Macleod was at the door, asking Ross to join them in the office. Once inside, Ross sat down beside Jona at the conference table where Macleod joined them.

'Show him,' said Macleod; 'show him.'

Jona had several photographs showing fragments of what was labelled as part of the grenade. 'It's been hard work, but we've managed to pull together different ones and we've got a part serial number.'

'Really?' said Ross. 'How on earth? That's not a normal photograph, is it?'

'No, it's not, but we have our ways,' said Jona. 'I had to send it away to one of the universities, but I had a faint suspicion. I could see part of the inscribing, but now you have it: 0342. It looks like there's a significant number of digits before it, although most of them seemed to have been scored through. I can't give you anything better, sorry about that.'

Ross was almost off the seat looking at the numbers. 'No,

no, it's fine. That's fine,' he said.

'I take it that's of use to you,' said Macleod.

'Been trying to trace to see if anything's been stolen. Grenade, handgun, because that's what we know has been out there.'

'The weapon that you brought in,' said Jona, 'the serial number was taken off that handgun. They obviously knew it was a risk. I guess they thought different with a grenade. Well, boom, no grenade left. Doesn't quite work that way, but I'd say we've been pretty lucky.'

'I wouldn't,' said Macleod. 'I'd say you've been damn thorough as ever. Thank you.'

'I haven't got much else for you. The fuel that set Jai Smith on fire could have come from anywhere. The fuel in the car was the same type of fuel, but again, you could pick it up anywhere. The serrated bladed knife, again, I can't tell you where it's from, just that it's a large military knife.'

'You've done great, Jona, as ever,' said Macleod. 'Ross will get onto this.'

'How's Jane holding up?' said Jona. Macleod looked away. 'That bad?' said Jona, 'Maybe I'll drop down and see her.'

'Don't,' said Macleod, 'don't. She said she doesn't want to see anyone. I think it's best we let her rest.'

Jona nodded, stood up and left the room, leaving Ross with the photograph of the grenade fragments and the number written at the bottom.

'Oh, I better make a call,' said Ross. 'Angus sort of volunteered to go down and see Jane. I said it might be a good idea because . . . '

'Don't make that call,' said Macleod. 'He's with her, and I think he's doing good. It's quite funny, isn't it?' said Macleod.

'She's being looked after by the one person attached to this team that I didn't want to meet.'

'Why is that, sir?' asked Ross.

'You know why,' said Macleod. 'Took me a long time to get to know you and you're not . . . well, you're not like me, are you, in your tastes? You, I couldn't get away from, you're right in front of me and you're a darn good copper, but your partner, well, it took me a time to come round to him, and here he is helping my Jane out. Sometimes I forget the strength I've got in the team around me and the team around them.'

Ross went slightly red, stood up, shuffling his papers. 'Just happy to help, sir,' he said and found that was all he could manage. 'I'll go and find where this grenade's come from.'

'Thank you, Ross,' came the comment, as the door closed. Back in the main office, he sat down in front of the computer, and tried to look at some manifests that had been sent through, but realised that he needed to go to the source. Ross took his car and travelled out to the nearest military complex, where he was able to talk to one of the quartermasters. They advised Ross that he'd need more permission than simply a policeman's badge. Ross told the man to contact the senior quartermaster.

Once it had been established that Ross was to be afforded every accommodation and help, they quickly traced down all serial numbers ending in 0342. There were many different items from cookware up to weapons. Ross looked at the addresses of where various items were meant to be held and he saw the Tain range. It was the closest to Inverness that was on the list, so he advised he would start there.

'I wouldn't get your hopes up,' said the soldier. 'You see, the stuff's all there. It's on the system. You'll be looking for stuff that's disappeared. We haven't found anything with that number missing.'

'Maybe not,' said Ross, 'but I'll indulge the idea anyway.' As he left the building he thought, *Maybe that's because you don't know it's missing yet.*

Ross drove north to Tain, happy to be out of Inverness with all the troubles that were going on. When he showed up at the range at Tain, his arrival had already been advised and he was shown straight through and taken to the armoury.

A number of doors were opened, and Ross was escorted into a room where a large number of hand grenades would be held. He asked about the codes and a man walked forward, lifting off several cases from a rack.

'They'll be in here,' he said. 'We haven't got through to using these yet, but obviously, as you can see, they're stored very securely. It'd be quite difficult to come in here; you'd have to know what you were doing procedure-wise. You'd have to get the pass and you'd have to get in. You really would have to understand how we work. Wouldn't be easy.'

'If you actually had a pass, could you get in?'

'Well, yes, of course, but even then, you'd have to justify why you were here. People don't come into this room very often and we sign we've been in because it's to do with the stock, weapons.'

'Could I take a look at who's been in then, over the last, say, two months?'

'Of course,' said the man, 'but first I'll just show you the grenades because if you see that they're here, you're not going to need to know who's in, will you?'

Ross nodded at the logic, but something inside him told him that he would require to see the paperwork. The soldier assisting him flicked open the cases and moved back the lids.

'There you go,' he said, 'all present and correct.'

Ross looked down at the grenades that were stored there, kept separate from each other. 'It looks quite deep though.'

'That's because there's a second layer underneath.'

'Obviously I don't want to touch them,' said Ross. 'Could you show me underneath?'

'Okay,' said the soldier. 'Just to keep you happy.' Ross watched him pick up the layer above and then almost drop it. Below, there was a grenade missing.

'Shit,' said the man out loud, 'I need to contact the captain. This isn't good. This really isn't good.'

'Am I okay to stay here?' asked Ross.

'I'll only be two minutes,' said the man. 'Stay here.'

Ross stood for two minutes looking at the empty hole where a grenade should have been. In front of him on the table sat the first layer, as well as the box containing the layer beneath. He was inside a secure facility. *How would you get them out?* He thought of his former colleague, Kirsten Stewart. *Somebody like that could get them out, but why would somebody like that be involved in riots in Inverness?*

Within ten minutes, the place was a circus, officers running back and forward, people being hauled in and questioned. Amidst it all, Ross stood still taking in the surroundings. Eventually, he went up to the captain who was looking extremely sheepish.

'Can I get five minutes of your time? I know you're busy and I know it's a shock, but that grenade ended up on an estate in Inverness. It killed four people and it's part of my murder investigation,' said Ross. 'I need your time, and I need it now.'

'Of course,' said the Captain. He stepped outside into the corridor with Ross.

'I need to know who's gone in and out of that room over the last two months.' The captain turned and barked an order at someone and then turned back to Ross. 'I suggest,' said Ross, 'that you also check your handguns and your knives.'

'Why?' asked the Captain.

'I picked up a military handgun from someone who tried to kill me on one of the estates. We also believe that another victim was stabbed with a military-grade knife. Serrated, it would be large. The sort of things you guys can handle, but wouldn't be found normally on a street.'

The man's face was white, but he nodded and gave further instruction. An hour later, Ross was sitting in the captain's office, records in front of him. Beside him were two men, both of whom were responsible for the armoury, and both of whom had been in that room over the last couple of months. The captain was giving them a grilling.

'If I can just interrupt you,' said Ross. 'Our two gentlemen, have you been on the base over the last couple of weeks? Have you gone home?'

'We've been here. We've been here the last two weeks. We haven't left the base the last two weeks or beyond.'

'Look down at the times you entered the building,' said Ross, 'and I want you to think, really think, are those times accurate?'

Ross watched the two men grab pieces of paper, and start skimming through. He saw the eyes of one go wide.

'Captain, I wasn't here then. Look, I wasn't here then.'

'But your card's been used,' said the captain. 'Your card was used to open that storage unit.'

Ross looked over; the knife and the gun had been confirmed as being missing as well.

'Where were you?' asked Ross.

'That was one of the old reunions. A lot of us who went through as cadets, we got back together. It's a reunion that's called for and organised.'

'Who was it organised by?' asked Ross.

'Charlie, Charlie Meadows.'

'Mr Meadows is where?' asked Ross.

'Charlie works admin nowadays. I think he's down in Glasgow.'

Ross nodded. It looked like he'd been making a trip to Glasgow. 'Can you detain Mr Meadows, please?' asked Ross. 'He's a suspect in a murder investigation.'

'I'll have the MPs on him straight away,' said the Captain. 'Thank you, Detective Ross, and our apologies.'

'Don't thank me yet,' said Ross; 'we're not at the bottom of it.' Yet, Ross could feel the scent was getting stronger.

Chapter 20

That evening while Macleod was visiting Jane in hospital, Clarissa got hold of Kelly McKinley and asked to talk to the kids on the Knockmalley estate. Kelly advised they'd have to meet them on the street, but possibly somewhere in the shadows, as the kids were not keen to be seen talking to anyone. With Ross away, Clarissa needed to chase down where the money had been moving on the estate, why young kids were getting paid and exactly how the riots were being caused. Possibly she could get a line in, maybe a contact to chase up.

Clarissa thought she would dress up in a street fashion, try and blend in, but when she'd gone home and looked at her wardrobe, she realised it wasn't going to happen. Kelly McGinley met her on the edge of the estate and together, the women walked to an area of the park away from the main playground where there were overhanging trees.

On a park bench among the shadows were sitting several children who Clarissa would've put anywhere between eleven and fourteen. Kelly had explained that those older than these kids were not going to speak but also realised that the worrying development was that a lot of the younger ones were being used.

Clarissa caught the strange looks, this older woman coming to them with a large shawl around her, boots halfway up her shins, and some tartan trousers underneath. She gawped at their black tracksuit bottoms, the hoodie tops, and fought the urge to stop thinking about what the world had come to. Beside her, Kelly was wearing a hoodie, but somehow it looked more stylish, bright in colour, along with a pair of jeans that Clarissa thought she would've struggled to get into in her twenties, never mind these days.

'Are you the copper?' asked a small boy.

'I'm Detective Sergeant Clarissa Urquhart so, yes, I'm your copper and I'm worried that you guys are being played.'

'What do you mean, being played?' said another voice.

'We've been noticing amounts of money are changing hands, but the wrong way, or at least not the normal way,' said Clarissa, correcting herself. 'Usually, you guys are handing over money to people giving you pills, drugs, booze, all this stuff you're not meant to have at your age.'

'All the stuff you won't let us have.'

Clarissa wanted to point out that it was the law and not her specifically and as far as she was concerned, some of these kids, they could go and drink themselves half to death. She didn't have Ross's more generous outlook towards them.

'Whatever,' said Clarissa, 'the main thing here is somebody's paying you guys to riot. Somebody's paying you to pick up a stone and from what we've seen, it's good money. I'm not out of line when I say two hundred, am I?'

'Who's getting two hundred?' came a voice from the back. 'I only got one hundred.'

'I got a one hundred and these trainers.' Clarissa looked down, saw the white tongue of a pair of trainers sticking out, laces undone.

'Who's giving you them then?'

'None of your business, copper, because if we tell you that you're going to stop them doing it. Where am I going to get my stuff from then?'

'The point is, they're sticking you up the front. You need to understand that these people who are doing this are up against others who want to work on this estate. Others that want you to go and buy those other things that I don't condone. What those people will do when you're not buying what they're offering is to come in and sort it out. When they come in, they'll come and talk to you but not the way I'm doing. They'll beat you bloody. If you're lucky, they'll leave you alive. These guys paying you the money now, they'll clear out, they'll be ahead of the game, so really, I'm here to protect you.'

'Well, you do look like a gran,' said a voice at the back.

Clarissa wanted to march around and clip the young lad around the ear. Back in her day, if you spoke to an adult like that, you'd have got clobbered, but you didn't get to do that nowadays, so she just held her pose, grim-faced.

'But it doesn't take away what they'll do to you,' said Clarissa. 'I'm not here for the good of my health. I'm here because this rioting can't continue. At some point they'll come in, they might even send the military in, and you don't want to face those guys; they're not like us; they don't go easy. They panic and they pull a gun.'

She saw some faces looking at her with some anxiety and she realised she may have overplayed her hand. Military weren't like that, well, not as far as she was aware.

'I want to know where this money's coming from?'

'It's the new guys,' said a voice. 'There are a couple of new guys coming in. They came over and spoke to us several days back. They said to us, "Can you pick up a stone?" Told us where to go, where to cause some problems.'

'Did they give you specific times?' asked Clarissa.

'Yes,' said one boy, 'told us, "Go here, go around the back." One was at the church. We were throwing stones there and when we did that, the Community Centre went alight. The other time we were at the shop pelting it, and there was the other place that went alight.'

A friend jumped in front of him, as they all started to seem excited to boast about what they'd done. 'Then we went over the Walmsley Estate, and we were told to run around, chase everybody away, and then that guy got killed, Smith, wasn't it?'

'Jai Smith' said Clarissa. 'You were given money to what? Run a different direction?'

'Well, no, we ran down past where he got killed and then up the other side; somebody said he took a wrong path.'

'They also said one of our guys did it from over this estate. Nobody's said who it is though.'

One of the girls came up from the back, she must have been thirteen at most, and she stood in front of Clarissa, holding a butterfly knife. 'I got given this, told to brandish it and run around with it. They said they'd give me one hundred pounds if I could get on camera.' She pulled a wad of notes somewhere in her back pocket. 'It wasn't difficult; cameras were everywhere, looking to film us all the time.'

'You decided to wield a knife on camera for a couple of hundred pounds, when in fact, you've actually just been caught brandishing an offensive weapon on an estate with a riot going on, so by public record, we could lift you for that. We've got the evidence; it's been on TV.'

The girl's face dropped. 'That's the problem, you guys; you're getting set up. Do you understand me?'

Clarissa surveyed the crowd. That's when she saw Kelly's jaw drop and her arm lift up, finger pointed. Clarissa turned around and saw a figure not that far away with a hooded top on and in their hand was a knife. It wasn't like the butterfly knife Clarissa had just been shown. It was bigger, thicker, like something a Marine would use. Clarissa turned to the kids, 'Run!'

They looked at her at first and she screamed at them. 'They're from the other estate!'

The kids looked at her, saw Kelly begin to run, and together they all fled across the park. Looking behind her, Clarissa saw the figure begin to run after them.

'Where are we close to? What's the nearest building?'

'Sports hall. Just over there,' said Kelly. 'Come on.'

'Is it not going to be locked?' said Clarissa.

'I have a key. I'm there every other Wednesday. I'll get us in. Let's go. Johnny,' she shouted as one boy went to run off a different direction, 'stick with us. Come on.'

Clarissa, who was definitely keeping at the rear of the group, turned and saw the person behind her, less than thirty yards away. Clarissa turned back, saw Kelly opening a door, and sprinted in after the kids. Kelly locked it while Clarissa looked around and shoved a small sofa towards it. The sports unit had only enough room for two badminton courts. There was a small changing facility area, but there was no other space within it, except for some small storage cupboards.

'We use it for small gatherings and that; it's not big.'

Clarissa noted that there was a small ladder facility that climbed up towards some lights at the top, and beyond that, she saw some windows.

'Where's that lead to?'

'Never been up there,' she said, and Clarissa immediately started to climb the ladder.

'What are we going to do? They're going to be outside there.'

'I'm going to phone and they'll come and get us,' said Clarissa, 'it won't be a problem. I just want to see what's going on.'

Clarissa continued her climb and as she reached the windows at the top, she stared down to see the figure that had pursued them. There was no one else around, but the figure had a large can of what looked like petrol. Certainly, some sort of liquid being tossed over the side of the building.

'They're pouring stuff over what looks like the wooden bit to the side of the sports hall. How old is this thing anyway?'

'This has been here over forty or fifty years; it's not in great shape.'

'Is the outside wood?' asked Clarissa, looking down at a slightly sloping roof with some corrugated iron across the top of it.

'There's a lot of wood in here. Why?'

'Gather the kids together. We may have to move quickly.' Clarissa began to dial the station number, calling the desk sergeant and immediately asking for assistance. As she did so she saw the side of the hut go up in flames. The flames spread right around it. Presumably, having had their path laid out for them by the generous coating of whatever fuel had been used to douse the building.

Clarissa asked for the fire service as well, advising they were trapped. She looked out of the window and the figure was still there, knife in hand, almost daring them to come out.

'They reckon we're going to break through the door,' said Clarissa.

Smoke started to pour in, thick choking smoke coming off the wood and rising up to the ceiling. Clarissa began to cough but clambered down the ladder looking for another way out.

'We can't come out this way,' said Kelly. 'If you're saying they're outside, as soon as we open anything here, they'll come for us.'

Clarissa went down on her knees as the smoke began to fill the hall. 'What else is beside here? Is there anywhere we could jump onto?'

'There's a roof just across. Did you see it in the dark?' It was a young lad speaking. 'I know because we've got up on that corrugated roof before and we've jumped across.'

Clarissa looked at the flames, wondering if the doors would soon burn in and whoever was outside would have access to them anyway.

She counted the number of kids with them. There were eight.

'Cover your faces as much as you can. Try not to breathe in too much smoke. We all climb the ladder and we go out through that window. Kelly, you go first. I'll bring up the rear.'

'We're not going to have enough time,' said Kelly.

'We won't if you keep gabbling. Let's go.'

Clarissa watched them begin to climb, the kids scampering up the ladder in a fashion much quicker than she could. The young lad who had suggested the idea was right behind Kelly who took the lead. She watched the window being opened and heard a banging at the door they'd come in. Someone was trying to kick it through, now the flames were destroying it.

Clarissa began to climb the ladder but could barely see through the thick smoke. As she reached the top, she stuck her leg out of the window where the smoke was now piling out, trying hard not to cough lest she gave her position away. She followed some kids along the side of the building to a small ledge that allowed them to drop down onto the corrugated roof. As she looked at them, she saw them jumping across.

Clarissa made her way down, stood carefully on the roof, and could feel the heat coming through it. She braced herself, ready to jump across a gap that in her heyday would've been no more than a skip. As she stepped forward, pushing down her left foot, she felt the roof begin to give away. She gave herself enough of a push that she was able to throw her hands out, grabbing the new ledge.

'Get me up,' she shouted and found Kelly telling the kids to grab an arm each. As Clarissa got pulled up and dragged onto the roof, she heard a shot. She didn't feel anything. Nothing was hit, but she rolled, telling the kids to stay down.

She could see the fear now in their eyes and she pulled them together. She instructed Kelly to keep them down low and in the middle of the roof. On her backside, Clarissa edged over to the corner where they had jumped across. If the figure was going to come up it would come from there. Clarissa waited, one knee pulled back, her foot ready to kick out. She heard police cars in the distance and then a head appeared following two hands that had just clambered onto the roof.

Clarissa kicked hard. She watched the figure drop to the ground. Almost instinctively, she clambered to the edge to look down. It was a stupid thing to do for they had a gun, but Clarissa did it without thinking. Then, when she saw the figure getting up gun in hand, she knew she was an obvious target, so she simply fell off the roof landing on top of them. The person broke her fall, but still, the ground came up fast.

She reached out with her hand, grabbing the hood of her attacker. Then something was in her hand. She had grabbed the hood off them, and now their hair was displayed. They weren't daft enough to show their face but the brunette hair had distinct blonde edges. Hair that ran down till it just touched the shoulders. Clarissa stared and missed the backhanded swipe that caught her across the side of the face. It wasn't a clean blow, but it knocked her backwards.

The sirens were now filling the air and there were cries of police officers. The heat from the fire beside her drove her to cover her face as she watched the silhouetted figure disappear into the night.

It's a woman, she thought. *It must be a woman.*

Chapter 21

Macleod could smell the scene of the escape before he saw it. The fire service had doused the fire and a little distance away he saw his sergeant being checked over by a paramedic. She looked flustered, but there was also that steely determination he'd come to know from Clarissa. As he got close, the smell of smoke from her shawl and trousers almost overwhelmed him.

'I said to go and investigate the estate. Find out what's going on. Not cause a fire in the process.'

'Whereas normally, I appreciate your humour, I think we're both well past it,' said Clarissa, her voice tinged with anger. 'It'd burnt the lot of us down if there hadn't have been an escape route up and out onto that corrugated . . . well, you can't see it, can you? It's gone. There was a corrugated roof there that we jumped across. The attacker shot up at us. I managed to kick them in the face when they tried to climb up on that roof and then I fell down on top of them.'

'That's why your shoulder's going to be tender for the next couple of days,' said the paramedic, 'but, as far as I can tell, you haven't put anything out. There's a bit of bruising, but really, they did break your fall. You might find they're a lot worse for wear.'

'Well, if they feel worse than me,' said Clarissa, 'they deserve it.'

'Did you find anything out though?' asked Macleod.

'Kids are getting paid. It's new people that have come in, ones they don't recognise, but they're handing these kids one hundred or two hundred, and then they're orchestrating them, telling them where to go on the estate. How to start the riot. They're also dragging people away. These murders are, in some sense, premeditated. Certainly, the one when the riot was on, they were coordinating where that rioting was going.'

'Coordinating it? So, they could get to Jai Smith?'

'Jai Smith, or just to get to someone. That's probably more like it.'

'And how is Miss McKinley?'

'Girl did well,' said Clarissa, 'kept her head, did as told. She cares about those kids a lot more than I do.'

'I didn't ask you to care about them,' said Macleod. 'We just ask you to do your job, which you did.'

'I had her though,' said Clarissa, 'I landed on her and I had her. If I could have just gotten up, got a hand around her . . . '

'You probably would've been dead,' said Macleod. 'As soon as you kicked her off that roof, you should have stayed up there, stayed safe.'

'I'd gone to the edge,' said Clarissa, 'and gone over, and she would've shot up at me. It was safer to jump.'

Macleod raised an eyebrow, 'As long as you're all right,' he said; 'next time, play it safe.'

'Play it safe, Seoras?' said Clarissa suddenly. 'They tried to burn us alive. We were going for our life. Play it safe? Sometimes you've got to confront these people. Sometimes you've got to . . . '

Macleod put his hand up. 'Okay, I get it. I get it. There's no good way out of this, but you're alive. Those kids are alive.'

'And I can also tell you the colour of her hair; brunette, long, down to the shoulder with blonde tinges at the end.'

'How did you?'

'Pulled the hoodie down. They didn't turn around, so I never clocked their face. They were almost too sensible for that, took a swipe at me, but they weren't looking so they caught my head, but not with the fist. More like their wrist knocked me to the ground. Then they disappeared off into the dark. They were quick. They jumped up onto the roof, were pulling themselves up. This person is fit, I mean, look at it, you and I couldn't jump up onto that roof without getting a leg up from somewhere.'

Macleod looked at it and he was sure that he couldn't; he doubted if Hope could or Ross. The sort of person who could have done it was Kirsten Stewart, the former constable that worked for him before leaving for the secret service. The thing about Kirsten though, was she had trained all her life; she'd been a mixed martial artist. She was incredibly fit and despite being smaller than he, could have jumped up to that roof no problem.

'So, we're looking at someone with training,' said Macleod. 'I'm getting the feeling this is a soldier. This is a soldier of some sort, but why? What on earth has a soldier got to do with all this? We need to check the estate. See if there are any soldiers living on the estate. See if they can account for their whereabouts, clock them for why they're here. What they think about the situation.'

'I could swear it was a female. The hair looked female. The build? Well, I'd have said it was a strong build, but I felt it was female. I know it was dark, Seoras.'

'We'll lean towards that way, but don't discount any men in case they're very lithe, slightly different figure. Get hold of uniform, ask for some assistance. Canvas the area, canvas the houses, see if we've got any military people living here. Also check for anybody who fits the hair description that you've said. They may not be military; they may just be interested in the military. There may be people who go down to gyms, people who are trained to fight elsewhere.'

'The orchestration though, it speaks of military, doesn't it? The ability to organise your plans beforehand, enact them while you act alongside.'

'If it's one person,' said Macleod, 'but this could be several people.'

'But that doesn't feel right, does it?' said Clarissa. 'We'd have broken into it by now. Somebody would've cracked, somebody would've said something, and why, if that was the case, would you go ahead and kill Jai Smith on your own? No, I clearly think this is an individual.'

Macleod turned away, breathing out to force away the smell from Clarissa's clothes. 'Go and talk to uniform, see if you can get that moving and then go home and get a bath.'

'I'll be back in a bit,' she said.

'I think you've done enough tonight,' said Macleod. 'You don't need to be.'

'Seoras, they went after your Jane; they've come after me. They've been after Ross. We don't rest on this one. We don't take time out.'

Hope McGrath suddenly joined the situation and looked at the fire. 'Certainly plenty of fuel. By the way, Ross called. He said he's got a lead on the grenade, the gun, and the knife.

They're all missing from the Tain range. One of the guards there seems to have access to the site, except he couldn't have because he was elsewhere, so credentials have been stolen.

'He said he's chasing a lead regarding questions asked at a conference, so Ross is trying to track that down, see if he can find a way in. The last he said, he was heading for Glasgow.'

'Well, let's hope he has more success than we've had so far,' said Macleod. 'Right, let's get tied up here, get to interview these kids and get them and Kelly back to their houses. I've had word that the Warmsley Estate's kicked off again.'

Macleod wandered the scene looking for anything, thoughts churning through his mind about who could be doing this. Military was coming to mind, especially now with what Ross had found but why? What was the point? What was the purpose?

The initial canvas throughout the area came back negative. They'd found three women who displayed the hair colours but they all had secure alibis. Macleod wondered if the person was even living here. They had disappeared off into the dark, Clarissa had said, but if they didn't live here, what was the point? Why were they doing this? What were they looking to show?

Now, Macleod had two lines of inquiry that were not meeting: rioting on an estate and murder committed on the estate, seemingly far apart except that one was possibly used as a smokescreen for the other. He remembered what Ross had said about the task force, about Macleod being brought on board for it. The swell of ground opinion, was that it? Were they looking to eradicate all issues? Is somebody daft enough to think that you could solve an estate like this by simply having a large task force turn up, charge in, and save the day?

He didn't believe it. He certainly wouldn't know where to start on that. It was a long time since Macleod had worked out on the street. His mind wasn't suited to that sort of thing; it was suited to seeing the motives of bad people; people that had been hurt, people that had been greedy, people that had to cover something up. He didn't know how to deal with disaffected youth. He'd never had kids.

It was three hours later when he next bumped into Clarissa and the woman smelt a lot better than she had before.

'Can't get it out of my hair though,' she said. She had clearly tried but she had a scarf around her head, something she didn't tend to do. It must have been bad as the image was not one she would have wanted to portray on the street.

Hope had reported back that she'd spoken to the young people. All had said very similar things to Clarissa. They talked about how they pulled her up, and she thought they had a greater respect for her since she brought them out to safety at the risk of her own life.

The search through the estate continued, and Macleod fielded a call from Jim, the Assistant Chief Constable, who advised him that he needed more of his officers on the Walmsley Estate. Macleod had thanked him for what he could do, said, of course, he could have whoever he needed at this time. He spoke to Jona who had arrived on scene but the woman had nothing for him. She had hoped there'd be a hair left behind, and in the dark they were combing the grass but it could have blown away by now if one had fallen, trampled into the ground. It would be difficult, and then you'd have to see if the DNA even came up with anyone.

At six in the morning, Macleod sat in another hall. This

time there were seven veterans in front of him. None of them matched the hair type that they were looking for and none of them seemed youthful enough for the activities that had been going on. It was another line of inquiry that was just dropping out.

He yawned and placed a call to the hospital where Jane was asleep. The nurse said she'd had a reasonably good day, but she was still nervous. He wanted to be over there with her, but he knew she'd just chase him. *Tell him to go and find that killer.* He'd also make her a good deal happier if he could do this.

Twenty minutes later, Ross rang, having made his way down through the night to Glasgow. He'd discovered the man he wanted to talk to, Charlie Meadows, wasn't there. Charlie had headed north, and Ross was making his way to a small outbuilding somewhere just south of Aviemore. He said he would call the Inspector as soon as he had something, and Macleod told him to hurry up.

Over in the Walmsley Estate, they were counting the cost of the night's rioting. A shop had been burnt out. There was fire damage to several places. Cars had been set alight, windows had been smashed here and there, and the place generally looked a mess. When Macleod spoke to Jim, the Assistant Chief Constable, he could hear the weariness in the man's voice. 'Find him, Macleod.' That was all he said, 'Find him.'

As it approached seven o'clock, Macleod decided that he would head back to the office, get a shower, and then start again, while he waited for Ross's report. As he made his way to the car his phone began to ring and he looked down to see Jim was calling him.

'Just about to leave,' said Macleod. 'What can I do for you?'

'More like what you can do for me. I think I've had an

attempted murder over here, young lad lying on the ground. He was hidden in one corner of the playground. Linda Donald, a local resident attracted our attention. We didn't see him at first because he wasn't moving. I don't know but I'm thinking this might have been the murderer.'

'On my way,' said Macleod. 'I'm on my way, Jim.'

Chapter 22

L inda was taking her morning walk down to the shops. She was fretting about it, worried that the trouble on the estate hadn't gone away. But so far, the early hours of the day seemed to be better for getting about without any trouble. Maybe they'd all gone home to sleep after rioting through the night. She looked around at the rubbish scattered here and there—stones and bricks lying on the road, crushed bottles.

She saw a council worker sweeping them up and gave the man a smile. He tried to force one back, but he looked miserable. *Not really what you signed up for*, she thought. She turned round the corner and heard a crunch, looked down, and saw glass that was broken underneath her feet. She was thankful she had her stout shoes on, not flip-flops.

She looked across to the shop, hoping that it had got through the night unscathed. It sat tucked in a small terrace. She saw that the shutters were still down over everything except for the front door. The shutters had taken a battering, but they were intact. She hoped that inside was as well.

Linda entered the shop and saw a sharp glance from Fazel, the owner.

'Oh, it's you?' he said. 'Morning, Linda. Papers are in.'

'Thank you, Fazel,' she said. 'Are you okay?'

'I slept upstairs last night. Had a baseball bat with me. Some things hit the door, but the shutters held. I had the back door barricaded as well and moved the fridge up against it. Not sure if that would've held it though. It's terrible.'

'It really is. I don't think they're any closer to stopping it.'

She walked down one of the small aisles and picked up a packet of croissants. Then her eye caught a bar of chocolate. She really shouldn't, but if she was going to be stuck in most of the day, why not? *In fact*, she thought, *maybe I should get a few more things in case I don't get out for a day or two*. Soon, Linda was walking back from the shop with two bags, and she'd only popped out for the croissants. Still, at least, she wouldn't go hungry.

Her flat was on the top floor, and she was glad of this, believing it would keep her safe. Although so far, the rioters hadn't generally come into people's houses, setting their anger against community fixtures, such as sports halls, and churches, anything that the council put up. She looked over at one of the speed cameras and saw that the top of it had been removed. There were probably plenty of motorists who were glad about that, but it still looked horrendous in the street.

Linda decided to take a walk through the park before going back to her house, reckoning that this was the only time she'd probably get to do it, and despite the heaviness of the shopping, she needed to take a chance to get a breather.

The buses were all askew now, many of the drivers not happy about coming through the estates, so the route had been cancelled at least to the end of the week.

As she entered the park, she saw several police officers,

highly visible in fluorescent jackets. She did wonder if the military would ever turn up as had been threatened on the TV. She'd seen that man from the council, Mackenzie; he was everywhere on the television, calling for this or calling for that.

Linda thought something had to be done, but the man was so prominent. What had they done before? Nothing. Maybe it was because the estates got into this bad repair. Many of the fixtures that were now completely broken hadn't worked anyway. As for the play park, the young kids couldn't play on it because of the occasional needle left over, or broken bottle from last night's fortified wine or alcopop.

She trudged on until she saw the sign that said Knockmalley Community Hub in front of her. She saw a burned-out building. Two weeks ago, she'd been in there. It was bingo night, and it wasn't great, but it was a bit of fun and she'd walked out to it. True, she'd been sticking to the main roads, but it was safe enough and she'd walk back. Now, she didn't go out her door after teatime. In fact, the last couple of days, she hadn't even been out after lunch.

Linda gave a shake of her head and turned to walk to the far side of the park. From there, she'd turn back and go around two corners that would lead to her flat. That would be her walk for today

She stopped for a moment, went to take in the fresh air, and realised that all she could smell was the charring. She listened intently, hoping to pick up the sign of some birds. They were there. There was also something else like a murmur, a whimpering.

She tried to orientate where it was coming from and then strode off past a roundabout. Then towards some bushes, she stopped for a moment. Should she get the policeman to come and look? Yes, that would be more sensible. Wouldn't it? She put down her shopping, turned, and walked back ten pieces until she could see one of the yellow-jacketed policemen.

'Oi,' said Linda, 'excuse me. Can you come?'

The policeman, once he realised she wanted his attention, bolted over. They were clearly on edge. As he ran past the charred wreckage of last fortnight's bingo, Linda could understand why.

'What is it, Ma'am? Can we help?'

'I'm hearing some murmuring. A sound. Can you hear it?'

The policeman stopped. Linda watched him close his eyes. She joined him. For a moment, she could only hear the robins, some distance away.

'I think it's coming from over there,' said the officer, and he moved forward into the bushes. Linda, the shopping still on the ground, followed him. She watched as he pushed back the shrubbery and there, underneath a tree, lay a young man. His face was black and blue.

Linda went to kneel down, but the officer told her just to remain back. As he started speaking on his radio, she heard him call for an ambulance and further assistance. Linda stood looking at the bloodied and bruised face of a boy she recognised. That was Anna's grandson. *He's only fourteen.* She shook her head but was then suddenly relieved when the officer managed to help the boy to a half-upright sitting position. As the boy tried to look up, one eye seemingly permanent closed, although it looked it like it was inflated like a tire, the other scanning around but unsure if it was actually seeing. There was dried blood in a line from his nose. Linda took a step back. *Poor Anna*, she thought, and some tears started to run down her face.

* * *

Hope pushed open the door of Macleod's office. 'What is it?'

'They found a boy beaten,' said Macleod. 'Jona is coming over in the minute. She was checking notes from the paramedics on scene, exactly what had happened.'

'But he's alive?' queried Hope.

'Yes, but I was wanting to check for an attempted murder in case our killer got it wrong,' said Macleod.

'Where did they find him?'

'Knockmalley Estate, just beyond the park in the shrubbery; local resident walking past called the police over, but he's gone to hospital.'

Both heads turned as they saw Jona Nakamura with her dark black hair tied up behind her marching into Macleod's office. 'Don't get excited,' she said, 'Boy is going to be okay, a bit of a doing.'

'A bit of a doing?' said Macleod. 'That's not a very professional term.'

'He received multiple blows in the head, plenty of contusions, but the only blood on him came from his nose.'

'What happened?' asked Macleod.

'Well, we don't know, do we?' said Jona. 'What I can tell you was they weren't trying to kill him; they were trying to rough him up. He's in the hospital, he's not in a great way, but he'll live. He certainly wasn't in danger of dying.'

'You think he got caught up in the wrong crowd?' asked Macleod.

'Hasn't happened yet,' said Hope, 'So far the rioters haven't turned on each other. In fact, they haven't particularly turned on the actual residents, have they? They've been setting fire to council property, things that represent institutions on the estate. The woman that got her house ransacked, that actually was quite an outlier; the real damage has been done to fixtures, and once the police are on scene, we're getting attacked like anything. Now this seems a bit strange, Seoras.'

Macleod watched Hope sit down in a chair, mind clearly ticking over.

'If there's nothing else,' said Jona, 'I need to get back on to the rest of my cases. There're several things out there getting checked over. We're trying to see if we can pick up anything that's linking into our murderer.'

'Thank you, Jona,' said Macleod, and watched as she made her way through the door. He then turned to Hope, 'What?'

'I need to pay a visit,' she said, 'I need to check what this is. I don't think this is our murderer.'

'Okay,' said Macleod.

'I'll be back,' she said. 'It'll only take me half an hour.'

Hope drove to the outskirts of Inverness, once again entering the posh estate with its large five-bedroom houses. As she approached the door with the large pillars on the other side, she saw the two large men who stepped across in front of the door.

'I'm here to see Mr Burns,' said Hope. 'He needs to talk to me.'

One of the large men rapped the door. It opened on the small individual who had come out previously to Hope. He sneered at her.

'I need to speak to Mr Burns; it's urgent.'

'Mr Burns speaks to who he wants to speak to. I'm not sure

he's at home.'

'Maybe I can speak to Mrs Burns.'

'Mrs Burns is still on holiday,' said the weasel-like man, at which point Hope stepped forward.

'Then Mr Burns is in. Part of the deal last time was he was looking after the kids while she was away. Kindly ask Mr Burns to see me.'

She noticed that the two burly men had stepped further into her path, but Hope didn't back down. She wished Kirsten Stewart was with her; the girl had been great fun to have about because she never felt intimidated by anyone else. She was a tiny figure, but she packed a punch that could beat the best of them.

The weasel-like man reappeared a few minutes later and Hope found herself in the sunroom at the back of the house. Beyond it, she could see kids playing in the pool again, a nanny of some sort looking after them. Mr Burns was dressed in a suit.

'When I spoke to you last time, Sergeant, I wasn't expecting you to come to see me again.'

'I wasn't expecting you to be active on the estates either,' said Hope. She saw the man's face flicker.

'Who's saying I'm active there?'

'Things have got out of hand. Fourteen-year-old? Come on.'

The man said nothing for a moment. 'I think if you're going to come with that tone, we'll have to speak with my lawyer present.'

'No, we don't need to do that,' said Hope. 'If you come in like this, you're going to get all sorts of investigation. You might even get the whole riot thing stuck on you. We're going to get pressed to look at a murderer in your camp. We're not far away; we're close. Things will settle down again once we name who they are. I'm telling you to back off.'

'You're telling me?' said Burns. His face began to grow red. 'You don't tell me what to do.'

'I could march in here, I could tell you, and it could cause an absolute stink. This isn't something you're going to want. I can't arrest you for the murders because frankly, you didn't do them, but one of your guys beat up a fourteen-year-old; all that's going to do is fuel the mob. You're not going to control this one. Do you understand?' said Hope.

The man went up close to Hope, putting his face into hers. 'I'll bring them to heel.'

'No, you won't,' said Hope. 'You can't. We can't, no one can. We could bring the military and it wouldn't do any good; it would just raise the issue. The stakes would go up; more and more people will come. We need to diffuse this by finding our killers. Do you get that?'

The man raised his hand, his fist clenched and Hope thought he was going to hit her but then he opened it and ran his hand across her cheek. He stepped back, gazing at her.

'Macleod knows how to pick his deputies, doesn't he? You make sense but I can't leave it too long either. Twenty-four hours,' he said. 'Twenty-four hours. Then I'll have to take measures into my own hands.'

'You don't want to do that.'

'Of course, I don't, but the wife's back in twenty-four hours. Until then, I can't give it my full attention when it all goes crazy. Whatever happens at the other end, people will still want their bad habit. They'll still come to me.'

'Twenty-four hours,' said Hope. 'Stand down all your men.'

The man nodded, turned his hand towards a decanter of

whisky, poured himself one, then looked to offer Hope one.

'I told you before I'm on duty.'

'You ever think of coming to work for someone like me?' asked the man. 'We can give you most of what you want. Pays better than what you get now, less hassle. You'd command the respect of many people.'

Hope walked to the door then turned back and looked at the man, 'Just so you understand. You ply people with drugs they can't afford, you exercise control over people, ruin lives, and you've just beaten up a fourteen-year-old and you turn and offer me a job? If you didn't have somebody to clean it up, I'd spit on your floor.'

She turned and marched away from the door, pushing the weasel-like man away as he came rushing up towards her.

As the front doors were opened by the large men, she walked past with a comment to the pair of doormen, 'Go and get a proper job.' Without stopping, she marched to the front seat of her car, sat down, turned on the engine, and drove until she was clear of the estate. She pulled over into a lay-by and stopped.

Her hands were shaking. She just said that to Johnny Burns. She took several deep breaths. *Clarissa must be rubbing off on me*, she thought. Hope turned the engine back on and drove to the station. Twenty-four hours. They had twenty-four hours to solve these killings.

Chapter 23

Ross found himself just north of Aviemore at an address given to him for Charlie Meadows. The man was still working within the military but was on a weekend off. The address hadn't been very forthcoming. Ross had been talking to one of the captains located at a barracks just outside Glasgow. All he knew was that Charlie Meadows was on leave. But when Ross pushed, talking about the situation on the estates, the captain, having seen the trouble on the television, decided to go through his men and find where Meadows had gone. It had taken an hour or two, but Ross had been impressed by the intensity shown by the captain.

Charlie Meadows had a wife and one of his colleagues said that she wasn't aware he was on leave. It had taken another colleague to come up with an address, somewhere Charlie had hired north of Aviemore. As Ross had driven up from Glasgow, the one thing he thought was at least the man wasn't going to go far. You don't disappear for a dirty weekend, and then go on a thirty-mile hike.

Ross saw the track that led to the small cabin with a stunning view over a loch. He turned the car in to see two cars already there. One was small, but very new, a hatchback of some sort.

The other was an old beaten-up car, and Ross was able to identify it as that owned by Charlie Meadows.

Stepping out of his own car, he walked up to the front door of the log cabin and banged on it. As he stood in the silence, he could hear the birds chirping and feel the cool breeze blowing off the loch in front of him. The day was bright, the sun was out, and it certainly looked like an ideal location. He'd expected something more sordid, but clearly Charlie was there to impress.

When he got no answer, Ross banged on the door again. As he stood listening, he thought he could hear the loch bubbling. He looked around for the trickle of water entering it. It would come off some rock or a small waterfall. He stepped away from the door closer to the loch, but then realised the sound was coming from behind.

Ross thought he heard a whisper, again from behind the house. He was operating against a killer, so he was being cautious, and instead of going straight to the rear of the house, he skirted at some ten meters, close to the water. The water extended to a patio, and he could see a Jacuzzi on it. The penny dropped.

Ross climbed the small hill up and saw two figures lying low in the water; one he recognized from a photograph as Charlie Meadows.

The other one was a young woman. Ross stopped when he thought about the description he was giving her. Was it a girl? Charlie Meadows was in his forties. The age gap here was . . . well.

At first, Ross thought the man had hired himself a hooker, but then he thought about the car outside. Was she a rich girl? The car she'd arrived in was more expensive than his and although Ross didn't skimp, he certainly wasn't able to afford that price bracket of car.

'Charlie Meadows. I need to ask you some questions. If you'd kindly step out of the Jacuzzi, we can speak inside.'

'Who are you?' asked the woman.

Ross was already reaching into his jacket to pull out his ID. 'I'm Detective Constable Alan Ross from Inverness. And who are you?'

'Ashley,' said the girl.

'Well, Ashley, if you'd like to get out of the Jacuzzi, I may have questions for you as well.'

'I don't think so,' said Ashley. 'I'm not getting out.'

Ross had stepped a little bit closer to the Jacuzzi, and he suddenly realised that the water was stilling, Charlie Meadows having switched off the bubbles. It was at this point, he realised the impropriety of stepping out of the Jacuzzi. He looked around for towels or at least robes. There were none to be seen

'Okay, said Ross, 'I'm going to go inside, see if we can find something. You two are not going to run. The last thing you need to do is to disappear off naked in a car. You will get spotted. Stay in the Jacuzzi, Miss.'

Ross went inside and spotted a t-shirt and some pants clearly belonging to Charlie Meadows. He looked over what the girl had been wearing, saw a jumper and a long skirt. He picked them up, taking them outside and placing them on the patio. Charlie Meadow stepped out, shook himself down before pulling on his pants and his t-shirt.

'We'll step inside, ma'am,' said Ross, 'but follow us straight in once you're dressed.'

Ross motioned for Meadows to make his way inside. When

the man did, he turned and looked out of the window.

'You've just spent how long with her,' said Ross. 'You don't need to be doing that. Sit down. I've got questions.'

Charlie Meadows didn't move. Ross went over and grabbed him, giving him a short pull, bringing him closer to the seat. 'Sit down. Your commanding officer won't be happy if I tell him you didn't cooperate. It was a heck of a job to find where you'd gone.'

Meadows looked up. 'You what? You've been down at the . . . You involved him?'

'I did. I'll involve him further if you don't sit down and answer some questions.'

Meadows looked a little shocked and then he smiled. 'You can't blame me though. Can you?'

'I can blame you,' said Ross, 'and I am checking that woman's ID. If she's not legal, you are hauled in.' Charlie looked at him, suddenly worried.

'She said she was legal. I didn't quite ask it in that fashion, but she never . . . '

The door opened and Ashley walked in. Ross could appreciate that she would turn a man's head if he were so inclined, but he calmly pointed the chair opposite, asking Ashley to sit down. 'If you don't mind, I'd like to see your ID.'

'She came in a car. She came in a car.'

'Whose car is it?' asked Ross. Ashley pulled some ID out. It was a Scot card, not a driving license. 'Do you have a driving license?'

Ross looked down at the Scot card and saw the date of birth on it. 'The good news, Mr Meadows, is I won't be bringing you in for having sex with a minor. The disappointing news for Ashley is she will be getting arrested for driving a car without a license.'

Charlie Meadow's face dropped, 'No way,' he said. 'No way.'

'Enough,' said Ross, 'I need you to talk to me. There's been items taken from a military base. It appears that your pass has been used. I want to know where these items are.'

'I don't have the items,' said Meadows, 'and I don't know what you're talking about.'

'Tain Range. When were you last there?'

'It's been a while.'

'Your pass is valid and it was used to access a store room.'

'That pass is missing. It was missing for a while. I have reported it.'

'When did it go missing?'

'A while back. It was three, four days ago I called it in. Maybe they haven't got round to cancelling it yet. I thought they'd be quicker than that.'

'What happened when it went missing?' asked Ross.

'Funny enough, it was here,' said Charlie. 'I'd come here.'

'With Ashley?'

'No, it wasn't Ashley. It was someone else.'

The girl looked over him. 'You what, you just bring people here all the time?'

'Well, yes. I mean it's what you women like, isn't it?' The girl was disgusted and turned away. Ross hadn't time for this tiff and certainly didn't want to get involved into who had led whom on.

'You were here, and you lost it here. Have you searched the place since?'

'Of course, I did. I kept it quiet for ages until I couldn't find it. I've searched everywhere. It's not here.'

'Did you know that it definitely came here?'

'It was. It was in my pocket when I came down. It was only a brief liaison we had down here, but I asked her, and she hadn't seen it either. Hadn't picked it up by mistake.'

'Who's her?' asked Ross.

'Mackenzie. I mean she's left now. Couldn't believe it,' he said. 'I'd always liked her, but she was never interested. She'd been up at that base for a while and then she was leaving and she said to me, "How about it?"'

'She came onto you?' said Ross.

'No need to sound surprised. Happens with all the women.'

'Yes, right,' said Ashley, 'Pig.'

'Mackenzie? What's her full name?'

'Sarah Mackenzie,' said Charlie. 'Sergeant Sarah Mackenzie. Some operator; apparently, she'd been special forces. Done some dark operations and things. Certainly knew how to handle weapons, but she got married to some politician. She was staying there for a while within the military and then she left. She was complaining about it, said there was other work to do. To be honest, I wasn't really listening to her. She's telling me all this while she's on the job with me. What dame does that?'

'Is that just what we are?' said Ashley. 'Just something to be looked at and to . . . '

Ross put his hand up. 'I know you're probably hacked off at this man, but I have a murder investigation and I need to be asking the questions, so please, quiet. Sarah Mackenzie, you say; she can operate weapons?'

'Oh yes,' said Charlie, 'better than I can.'

'She was up at the base in Tain, the range?'

'She'd been based there for about three months. Not quite sure what she was doing. I remember she was asking me about

201

my job, because at the time I was doing a lot of the stores, inventory and things. She was asking how we could get in. I told her I had a pass, but that wasn't difficult to work out. Everybody knows that eventually.'

'How long did she spend down here with you?' Said Ross.

'That was it. I think it was a day. One night, she was gone in the morning, said she had to get back before her husband would notice.'

'What about after that?'

'Well, I rang her when the card was missing, but she said she didn't have it, never thought more of it. What do I do? I reckon she just wanted a quick one before she went off back to her husband properly. For all I know, she could have been having many of the guys up there. That sort of girl, the one that you want.'

Ashley stood up, marched over and laid an almighty smack across the man's face. 'I'm off home.'

'You're not,' said Ross. 'You're sitting there because you can't drive. Excuse me, no fighting.' Ross walked outside, looked at his phone, checking if there was a signal and rang Macleod.

'Sir.'

'Yes, Ross; Macleod here. What?'

'You're never going to believe who's in the military. Simon Mackenzie's wife, Sarah.'

'Okay. So?'

'The weapons that were stolen up in Tain. I found Charlie Meadows, the man whose card was used. Guess who slept with Sarah Mackenzie for a night several months ago and whose card went missing? He's kept it quiet until very recently.'

'Are you in front of a TV, Ross?'

'No,' he said, 'I've been driving all day; why?'

'I'm sat watching the Knockmalley Estate about to erupt after finding a fourteen-year-old beaten heavily, and Simon Mackenzie's being interviewed in front of his house, telling everyone about the need for a high-profile figure like me to take charge.'

'Still at that, sir? What are you going to do?'

'Get in your car and join me at Simon Mackenzie's house. I'm going to take charge, Ross. I'm going to lead the public and show them what's being done here.

Chapter 24

Macleod sat in the car while Hope drove along the Inverness streets to what was a more resplendent part of the town. Here, the houses reminded Hope of the ones she'd visited when talking to Burns, but someone such as him would never be in an area like this. This was truly respectable, and Councillor Mackenzie had a profile to keep up.

As Macleod pondered on the situation, his thoughts went to his partner Jane still in the hospital and hoping to be released later that day. He'd end up spending tonight in a hotel, or at least she would, if he didn't get this case closed. He was probably going to be up again into the early hours of the morning. But now, they had a chance.

All evidence pointed to Sarah Mackenzie having taken the weaponry that was being used on the estates. She was a trained soldier. It fitted with the way planning had been implemented and with the weapons that had been used, but it still had to be proved. There was no link, no direct link to Sarah. The case could be made that Charlie Meadow's access had been taken, but unless she had it, they couldn't prove she took it. A mere set of coincidences.

There was also the minor issue, but she hadn't been seen on the estate. Now, arriving with a show of force, Macleod was second-guessing what he was trying to achieve, knew he was operating outside of his norm, but the stress it had put on him, the damage it had done to Jane, for once in his life, Macleod wanted someone to pay, not simply to catch the culprit.

As he neared the house, he saw the media sprawled along the street, satellite dishes on top of cars, ready to feed back a statement from Councillor Mackenzie. The estates were in uproar again, mainly due to the beating of a child and an incident that had nothing to do with the murders.

'You'll need to pull in here, Hope,' said Macleod, pointing to a spot on the street. 'We're not getting any closer.'

'You sure you want to do this with all the media here?'

'If this works out, everyone will see. There'll be no cover-up.'

'If what works out? Are we going in to arrest her or we're just bringing her in for questioning?'

'We need to find evidence,' said Macleod, 'but we need to catch her unawares. If we come in later, having forewarned them, there'll be nothing here. Everything will go to ground. She'll cut contacts. That's if it's her, of course. She may just be the killer. Who knows how the rest of it's organised?'

Hope had reported twenty-four hours was all that Johnny Burns was giving. If Burns went and attacked the place, who knew how far the death toll and the number of beatings could reach to. Macleod could see the military being deployed. As much as you appreciated what they did in life, this was an estate in his adopted city. This was not somewhere that the military should be.

Macleod marched along the street, Hope, almost racing to keep up with him and the rest of the team. As Macleod approached the house, he saw Mackenzie standing at the edge of the drive, giving a TV interview, and then his hand went up shouting over to Macleod.

'And here's the man himself. The man we need to turn this all around.'

A reporter took a mic and shoved it into Macleod's face. He could see the camera on him and knew what the DCI would've wanted him to do; time for a reassuring message, time to let everyone know that things were under control, that he was going to sort it out. Well, they could forget that. His hand went up and shoved the microphone well out of the way.

'Councillor Mackenzie, where is your wife? She's wanted for questioning.'

Mackenzie's face was a picture, and it took him at least five seconds to rally. 'What on earth, Inspector? You can't be serious.'

'I'm very serious. Where is your wife?'

'We're just saying here how you were going to get to the bottom of things. I think that you've . . . '

'I don't want your thoughts,' said Macleod. 'Where is your wife?'

'She's around the back of the house. She's doing some gardening.'

Macleod turned to Ross and Clarissa. 'You two, round the back. Let me know what you think.' Mackenzie walked over to try and stop them.

'What's the matter?' asked Macleod. 'You worried about people going to talk to your wife? If she's innocent, you've got nothing to worry about. She's wanted for our inquiries.

'I was just going to tell her.'

'There's no need,' said Macleod. 'These two officers have

been attacked while on the estate by the same assailant. They know the rough size and build. I'm sure they'll be able to tell that assailant apart from Mrs Mackenzie.'

Once again, the man's face went white and Macleod hoped they were getting this on the cameras. He rallied terrifically though.

'How dare you? How dare you insinuate that my wife has had anything to do with it? How on earth can my wife have anything to do with these killings and why?'

Macleod turned away not entertaining the question, but he heard Hope step forward.

'A poor run for re-election so far,' said Hope. 'Be quite a feather on your cap, wouldn't it? Bringing in the man who calmed down these two estates. Things not going well in the polls for your re-election.'

Macleod pondered if Hope knew if any of this was true, as they hadn't discussed the man's electoral chances, but he decided to let it go and calmly strode down the side of the house, round to the rear. He was very aware that many camera crews were in pursuit.

'Inspector, Inspector, is Councillor Mackenzie's wife the killer? Is this who you're seeking? Inspector, we have a right to know.'

Macleod turned round, held up his hand, looked straight into the camera. 'We are pursuing inquiries at this time. Kindly let us be.'

He turned and continued to walk down the side of the house, knowing very well that having advised the media of this, there was no way they'd leave them alone. As he reached the rear, standing on the patio looking out into the garden were Ross and Clarissa. He could see them talking to each other. Then

Ross turned around and walked back to Macleod.

'It looks like she's the correct size and shape,' said Ross quietly.

'Good,' said Macleod also in a whisper, 'but this time tell me it out loud. There's cameras behind us.'

'I think we've got a match, sir. Looks like the same size and shape.'

'Very good. Let's get her for questioning, please.' Macleod turned round on his heel. 'Sergeant McGrath, can you not keep these cameras away? It's not an arrest we're making here. We're just looking to question someone.'

Hope for a moment looked somewhat shocked, but then put her arms up advising everyone there was nothing to see and could they disperse back out to the street. Of course, with that number of cameras, there was no way that Hope was going to be able to move them. Over his shoulder, Macleod could feel Mackenzie's breath.

'You'll not get away with this,' he whispered to Macleod.

'On the contrary, you won't get away with it.'

Macleod watched Clarissa talking to the woman at the far end of the garden and slowly, three figures returned, Ross flanking her on the other side. One thing that struck Macleod though was that the woman was dangerous, clearly capable of killing. If there was too much conflict, albeit direct, would she just lash out?

'Simon, what is all this? Why are these people coming for me?'

'We wish you to come in for some questioning about some missing weapons from a local army base,' said Macleod. 'I'm sure you'd be only too happy to assist.'

'This is outrageous. Simon, stop them.'

'Are you refusing to cooperate with inquiries?' asked Macleod, 'because we'd also like to search the house.'

'You'll not be searching this house without a warrant,' said Mackenzie.

A microphone was suddenly thrust in front of the man. 'Just confirm you're not happy for the inspector to search your house. Is there something to find, Mr Mackenzie?'

Macleod fought the urge to smile, but he turned around with a grimace and looked directly at the woman who put the microphone under the man's mouth. 'Did I not tell you to leave? Stop harassing Mr Mackenzie.' *That's my job*, thought Macleod.

The woman was undeterred and put the microphone back before the Councillor. 'So, Councillor Mackenzie, you actually think the inspector's going to find something. You said he was the man to get to the bottom of this. Why don't you at least let him try?'

There was a clamour and Macleod wondered how long the man could hold out.

'Simon, you can't let them through our home.'

'Why?' asked the reporter.

Macleod put his hands up again. 'I'd just like to say, can we calm it down, please? Can our press people please leave?'

Macleod heard the comment at the back which said that was not going to be very likely, but in a much coarser fashion. He ignored it completely and instead turned to face Simon Mackenzie.

'I wish to conduct an investigation. I wish to search your house to see, hopefully, if we can clear your wife from possible charges of theft from a government building. I'm happy to come back with a warrant if we need to. In the meantime, we might need more people to clear away this press contingent. I appreciate you may have something to hide that's not of a criminal nature, sir.'

Macleod thought Clarissa was going to snigger, but she took her wonderful laugh and turned it into a lighter smile, pulling out a multi-coloured handkerchief to hide her face. *Steady*, he thought, *guys, steady*.

Simon Mackenzie stood up in his crisp white shirt with the blue and white tie. He cut an imposing figure and he turned to Macleod and said, 'You can search away. I have nothing to hide. I doubt you'll find anything.'

The challenge was on. Macleod turned around to Hope and asked her to conduct a search of the premises, advising her to take great care that they didn't damage any of Mr Mackenzie's items. Hope walked towards the house and Mackenzie didn't flinch. When she disappeared inside, he still didn't. Macleod cast a glance at Mrs Mackenzie. She never flinched either. Macleod stood for twenty-five minutes until Hope emerged out of the house along with Clarissa and Ross announcing that nothing had been found.

'Are you happy then,' said Mackenzie, 'on what has been a gross intrusion on our privacy?' Cameras swung to Macleod.

'Don't forget to search the rest of the house, Sergeant,' said Macleod. He caught the glance from Simon Mackenzie to his wife, an involuntary flicker, to the right-hand side of the garden.

'Let's start with that greenhouse.'

Macleod saw the tremble in the hand and knew he'd hit bingo. This time, he marched down along with Hope, Clarissa, Ross, and the Mackenzies, and stood outside the greenhouse, the procession of cameras having followed him. He reiterated three times that they should leave and said he would call for backup, but he believed most of the uniformed officers were currently busy on the estate.

It was such a pity that they couldn't be used here at a time when they were needed. He made an impassioned plea for the press contingent to do the decent thing and step back at least to the pavement outside the house. There was no movement from them.

Ross went into the greenhouse with Clarissa and spent the next fifteen minutes searching. In the meantime, Simon Mackenzie had picked up his phone. Macleod knew where the call was going. It wouldn't be long before the DCI called him.

Macleod felt the phone vibrate. He reached down inside his pocket, slid the back cover off it and pulled the battery out letting all the pieces remain within his pocket. He saw Hope's phone begin to ring and she went to answer it, but Macleod advised her that she was on a search and not to be distracted. He said it so loudly that Ross and Clarissa took the hint and the next twenty minutes became a desperate search to find something, anything.

It was twenty minutes later when a man walked into the back garden, several uniform officers following him.

'What in the blazes, Inspector? What is this?'

'Just continuing investigations, sir. Mr Mackenzie has been good enough to allow us to search his house and his surroundings here in an attempt to clear his wife's name from a possible theft of military items. He is to be commended.'

Macleod could feel the sweat on his hands. This was getting too close. He was about to get a distinct order to stand down and leave. If he stayed, his career could be over.

'Well, Inspector, I think . . . '

Suddenly, the DCI had a microphone put under his face. 'Do you agree with the Inspector that there may be something here to find?' The DCI almost backed away. Another microphone came in. 'How do you feel about Mr Mackenzie's wife being implicated?'

'You were one that spoke up for his councillorship. Do you regret that now?'

The questions came in thick and fast, and the DCI was struggling to answer, but he seemed to rally under the gaze of Simon Mackenzie. He turned his back to him, and marched over to Macleod.

'This is a direct instruction,' said the DCI. 'You are to stop your investigation of these premises and return to the station to my office.'

'Is that right away, sir?' asked Macleod.

'Of course, it's damn well right away, and we'll talk about this, this insolence.'

'Of course, sir. You want us to pack up right now? Is that correct? I just don't want to pass out the wrong instruction,' said Macleod, desperately hoping his team could come up with something.

'Right now.'

Macleod turned, saw Hope on her hands and knees inside the greenhouse, Clarissa pulling at some grapes that were on the vine on the roof, and Ross outside, his hands underneath a compost bin.

'I'm sorry, team. I've being instructed by a senior officer that we have to stop the search, given his confidence in Mr Mackenzie and his wife. We are to return back to station.'

Macleod watched Hope stand up, Clarissa too, the disappointment and anger in their eyes, but then he saw Ross get up with a smile.

'I just found this bag in the compost bin. It's plastic. What's that doing there?'

'That's a special agent,' said Mrs Mackenzie. 'It's to help with the composting.'

'It feels like something almost furry inside. A lot of strands anyway,' said Ross. 'Shall I open it, sir?'

'We have to be careful; that could be evidence,' said Macleod. 'But our DCI has advised us that we are to stop. Do you want us to bring this in with us, sir?' asked Macleod.

The DCI's face was red like thunder. 'No. Let's go.'

'What's in the bag?' said one of the press. Suddenly, they were like vultures again. desperate to have a look.

'Am I to open it, sir?' asked Ross.

'No,' said Macleod. 'The DCI gave you a strict instruction.'

The cameras were again on the DCI. 'Are you sure this isn't evidence? What possible reason could you give for not opening this?'

The DCI was panicking and Macleod could see the sweat on Simon Mackenzie's face. The bag needed opened.

'Are you sure that what is in there, Detective Chief Inspector, isn't something belonging to a crime scene?'

'Just open the damn thing then,' said the DCI, 'so we can go.'

Ross pulled the bag apart, and from it produced a brunette wig. Macleod could have jumped in the air when he saw the blonde tips around the edges of it.

He saw Sarah Mackenzie look up at her husband, imploring him to do something, and he just shrugged his shoulders. She turned to run.

Ross saw her move first, stretched out a hand, but found

himself struck on the chin with the flat side of her palm, knocking him straight to the floor. Hope stepped across her but was also kicked hard in the stomach.

Clarissa was now on her way. As the woman looked to run to the rear of the garden, she stepped back a couple of paces, opening the way for the woman to run past. As she did so, Clarissa bent down and picked up a large stick. She flung it at the feet of the woman, causing her to trip and fall. Sarah Mackenzie's chin smacked into the ground, and she was momentarily stunned.

'Well, give me a hand,' said Clarissa. 'I can't do everything.' Ross got back to his feet, ran over and put a knee in the back of Sarah Mackenzie. With Clarissa's help, they handcuffed her, and Macleod called over to the uniformed police officers who had arrived with the DCI, telling them to arrest her along with Simon Mackenzie.

Almost immediately, the cameras converged. Macleod did his best not to smile. He simply turned and followed the Mackenzies as they were put inside police cars and taken away.

He turned to Hope. 'Organise the scene. Get this place thoroughly searched. See if we can come up with other weapons. It's still pretty circumstantial.'

'I'll get Jona down, see if we can get DNA off that wig.'

Macleod nodded and stepped inside the car. One of the uniformed officers was going to drive him, but as the car started to pull away, Macleod told them to halt. He could see Clarissa and Ross being instructed by Hope on what was to come next, but the picture that really delighted him was the DCI surrounded by press, badgering him for what had just happened.

Macleod tapped the chair, asking the driver to continue. He

waited until they got out of the estate. Then he allowed himself a full thirty seconds of belly laugh. As he brought himself back under his control, the officer in the front turned around and said to him, 'Anything funny, sir?'

'Nothing at all, Officer. Nothing at all. Am I understood?'

'Of course, sir,' said the officer in the front.

'It's not sir. It's Seoras. I don't mind being called Seoras.'

'Okay, Seoras,' said the driver, almost trembling, but careful to keep a stern and straight face all the way back to the station.

'Good man,' said Macleod. 'Good man.' He fought to contain the grin.

Chapter 25

Macleod shook the hand of Kelly McKinley and accepted the plaque that was handed over. He'd been against it. He told everyone there was no way he could accept this. It was a team effort.

'Then accept it on behalf of the team,' Hope had said. 'We got a win, we got a big win. The public needs to see we got a big win. You're going to put the police force on the map with this one, get confidence restored. The estates need to see it. They need to know this was all orchestrated by someone else, and it's not the youth on the estate or anyone else that's to blame for what happened.'

'A lot of that's not strictly true, is it?' said Macleod. 'Everyone's responsible for . . .'

'Oh, shut up and just take the award, Seoras,' Hope had said.

She'd walked off and he'd heard the swear, but he'd got the point. It struck him that she never would have said that, never in a million years, but she understood what was required, so she made sure that he understood as well.

Macleod smiled as best he could, and afterwards in the photographs, he insisted on Clarissa standing at the front with him.

'The older police officer has to be represented,' he said to her, at which point she gave him a mocking kick to the backside. A soft one, the one that let him understand that he'd been cheeky. It was all good fun, all a good release of tension, keeping each other happy, but underneath there was a current of loss. Jai Smith's parents had lost a son, Peter Olive's parents had lost their kid, and as for the four who had gone up in the car, well, that was something that would haunt their families for the rest of their lives.

They'd been thanks from the military as well, a visit from some bigwig. Macleod had let Ross take the brunt of the thanks. After all, he was the one that had chased that down. Maybe it suited them as well, having a photo opportunity with Ross, a gay police officer, along with the look of the new military, but that was all politics. Macleod didn't want to get involved in that. There were still other dark sides to think about.

Macleod came off the small platform and was embraced by a number of the local youth. He wasn't quite sure what they would say for he was very different in his dark suit and tie. One boy came up to him, barely able to reach up to Macleod's shoulders.

'I'm sorry,' said the boy. 'I'm sorry for what we did.'

'What did you do?' asked Macleod.

'Your wife,' the boy said. 'I'm sorry about your wife.'

'She's not my wife, she's my partner.'

'Well, I'm sorry for what we did.'

'What did you do?' asked Macleod, quietly to one side. The boy explained he'd been there, throwing stones, part of the chase. He hadn't been part of the gang exposing themselves and what they had done to Mrs Macleod had shocked him. Macleod nodded, thanked him for his apology, and watched the kid walk off.

'That's a touching moment,' said Hope. 'You handled that very well, but I know what you really thought.'

'I thought I wanted to string him up,' said Macleod, 'but change requires forgiveness, always. They're just kids getting led on. The real heroes here will be the ones getting this place back to its feet.'

'You could get involved in that. I mean, you just had the big thank you, Inspector Macleod ceremony. You could come around and do tree planting and all sorts of things,' said Hope.

'Don't mock,' said Macleod. 'The public eye has cost me. It's cost Jane more.'

'Is the house back to shape?' asked Hope.

'Completely. It's completely back.'

'So, when are you moving back in?'

'When she's ready,' said Macleod. 'When she's ready.'

'Back in the hotel tonight? Do you want me to come over?'

'It's okay, I think I can find my room,' said Macleod.

'You know what I mean. Can't be easy. Does she blame you for it?'

'She tries not to. There is a resentment, but she's a strong woman, Hope. She's found a new friend, though.'

'Who?'

'Angus, Ross's Angus. He's there just about every other day at the moment. She seems able to talk to him. In fact, last night, Ross and I were sat in the bar while Angus was up in the room with her. If I didn't know he was gay, I'd get worried.'

'She'll get over it,' said Hope.

'No, she won't,' said Macleod. 'She'll learn to live with it. She won't get over it. She never got over the acid attack. You might have saved her physically, but she never got over it. We might end up moving house. It's a pity. She wanted that house, but I think I'm the one that's grown attached to it.'

Macleod saw a figure walking towards him and recognised Jim, the Assistant Chief Constable. He was in uniform and shook Macleod's hand. 'You did good, Seoras. You did well. It was a bit of a gamble though, wasn't it?'

'Estates were getting out of control, Jim. It was all going to fall apart. Burns was coming in in the next twenty-four hours. Beatings were going to become commonplace. It would have all exploded.'

'You could have lost your job over it,' said the Assistant Chief Constable.

'I could, and so what? There was much more to be lost. As it is, only one person has lost his job.'

'Well, he didn't strictly lose his job, did he? Just moved elsewhere.'

'If all that Chief Inspector is doing is picking up paper clips and coating them, I don't care,' said Macleod. 'No right to be in a police station.'

'Quiet,' said Hope. 'There's cameras around. You can't say that out loud.'

'My minder,' said Macleod to Jim.

'No. She's the next Detective Inspector. When are you stepping up, looking for the exams?' he asked Hope.

'When I'm ready,' she said. 'I think I've got a few more things to learn off this man.'

'No, you don't,' said Macleod. 'Hope, you're ready. You've probably been ready for the last six months.'

'I'm not ready,' she said. 'I like the team. I like what we do, and I've got a man at home. Let me enjoy it for a bit.'

Macleod nodded and then walked away towards the middle

of the park. He could hear birds singing and looked over to where a hall had been burnt down. They'd done the best to clean up as they could, but it would still be a couple of months before they could come in and rebuild the hall. Builders had said it would be a rush job, but you can't rush things like that. Some things just take time to rebuild.

As he stood there, a woman came past carrying a shopping bag. She tapped him just below his shoulder and he turned, looking at a slightly older woman.

'It's the afternoon,' she said. Macleod glanced at his watch.

'It is,' he said. 'It is.'

'They said you put them away. I recognise your face from the telly.'

'We put them away,' corrected Macleod. 'It was a team effort.'

'I suppose so,' said the woman. 'You didn't get them for all the murders, did you? Is that correct? The press said that there wasn't enough evidence for that.'

'That is correct, but it looks like we'll get them for the four youths that died in the car. Peter Olive and Jai Smith, no, we won't. We'll try, but I'm not sure that will stick. The councillor, I'll get him on other charges, but he didn't actually kill anyone.'

'Okay, but you got him, yes?'

'Yes, I did, love. Thanks.'

'Well, well done. You know something; it's the afternoon.'

'Yes, it is,' said Macleod, 'It's the afternoon.'

'Tonight, there's bingo. We're going to go to the bingo.'

'Good,' said Macleod. 'That's nice.' He stood for a moment smiling at the woman, then looked away across the park.

'Well, thank you,' she said. 'Thanks again for the afternoon.'

As she walked away, Macleod saw Kelly McGinley coming over to him.

'Your sergeant said that you didn't do public relations very well. Is that right?'

'That's completely correct, Miss McGinley. I'm not like you. I'm not good at working face to face. I hunt down killers. I search through evidence. I give my team a kick up the backside to get things going. I get inside the heads of people whose heads you don't want to get inside, and I work like a dog to make sure it all comes out the other end. No, I don't do the public relations very well. Take that woman. She says to me, it's the afternoon, got bingo tonight. She said thanks. I actually told her, we'd get them, but knowing everything, and she just said thanks and then just kept telling me it was the afternoon.'

'During the time of the riots, she got out once a day if she was lucky. She was too scared. She's the lady who found the boy that was beaten up down here. She's saying thanks to you when she says it's the afternoon. She didn't feel safe enough to go for a walk in the afternoon, Inspector. That's her way of praising you. She didn't go to bingo either. They burned down the hall. Everything was taken away; it's coming back.'

'Well, good luck to you,' said Macleod. 'You've still got your work cut out.'

'We do, but Constable Ross is going to come down and talk to those kids. He's looking to take an interest.'

'Good on him,' said Macleod, 'because I'd wring their bloody necks.'

Macleod gave a wry smile, which made Kelly laugh, but deep inside, Macleod thought, *No, I really would.* Kelly moved on, but Macleod stood enjoying the sunshine and the birds twittering in the trees. He heard a baby laugh. A kid was playing in the play park.

'Are you ready to go?' said Hope.

'No,' said Macleod. 'Come here a minute.' Hope stood beside him, 'Suck it in,' he said. 'Feel this. This is the win. This is the win. Kids playing, adults out when they weren't before. This is the win.'

'Okay, Seoras, this is the win. Enjoy it.'

'No,' he said. 'Really enjoy it. I'm about to go back to a hotel room, to my partner who's scared stiff of going back to her real home. Might come to you one day if you become an inspector. It may come to you even if you don't. Suck it in,' he said. 'Enjoy it.'

Hope stood for a moment, then she turned, called over Clarissa and Ross.

'Don't rush me,' said Macleod.

'Who's rushing?' said Hope. 'You just taught me something. I want to make sure they understand, too.'

Read on to discover the Patrick Smythe series!

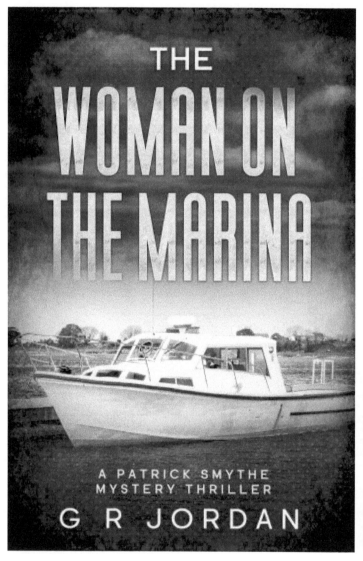

THE

WOMAN ON THE MARINA

A PATRICK SMYTHE
MYSTERY THRILLER

G R JORDAN

Start your Patrick Smythe journey here!

Patrick Smythe is a former Northern Irish policeman who

after suffering an amputation after a bomb blast, takes to the sea between the west coast of Scotland and his homeland to ply his trade as a private investigator. Join Paddy as he tries to work to his own ethics while knowing how to bend the rules he once enforced. Working from his beloved motorboat 'Craigantlet', Paddy decides to rescue a drug mule in this short story from the pen of G R Jordan.

Join G R Jordan's monthly newsletter about forthcoming releases and special writings for his tribe of avid readers and then receive your free Patrick Smythe short story.

Go to https://bit.ly/PatrickSmythe for your Patrick Smythe journey to start!

About the Author

GR Jordan is a self-published author who finally decided at forty that in order to have an enjoyable lifestyle, his creative beast within would have to be unleashed. His books mirror that conflict in life where acts of decency contend with self-promotion, goodness stares in horror at evil, and kindness blindsides us when we at our worst. Corrupting our world with his parade of wondrous and horrific characters, he highlights everyday tensions with fresh eyes whilst taking his methodical, intelligent mainstays on a roller-coaster ride of dilemmas, all the while suffering the banter of their provocative sidekicks.

A graduate of Loughborough University where he masqueraded as a chemical engineer but ultimately played American football, Gary had worked at changing the shape of cereal flakes and pulled a pallet truck for a living. Watching vegetables freeze at -40'C was another career highlight and he was also one of the Scottish Highlands "blind" air traffic controllers.

These days he has graduated to answering a telephone to people in trouble before telephoning other people to sort it out.

Having flirted with most places in the UK, he is now based in the Isle of Lewis in Scotland where his free time is spent between raising a young family with his wife, writing, figuring out how to work a loom and caring for a small flock of chickens. Luckily, his writing is influenced by his varied work and life experience as the chickens have not been the poetical inspiration he had hoped for!

You can connect with me on:
- https://grjordan.com
- https://facebook.com/carpetlessleprechaun

Subscribe to my newsletter:
- https://bit.ly/PatrickSmythe

Also by G R Jordan

G R Jordan writes across multiple genres including crime, dark and action adventure fantasy, feel good fantasy, mystery thriller and horror fantasy. Below is a selection of his work. Whilst all books are available across online stores, signed copies are available at his personal shop.

Rogues' Gallery (A Highlands & Islands Detective Thriller #21)
https://grjordan.com/product/rogues-gallery
Foreign royalty found dead on an island estate. A fractious gathering provides a plethora of suspects. Can Macleod and McGrath sort the treasure from the driftwood to reveal who truly gains the most from the duke's death?

DI Seoras Macleod is ordered away from his recovering partner Jane, to investigate the suspicious death of a foreign duke at the estate of his mother. Found naked and deceased in a small loch near the family's holiday estate, the duke is not short of enemies at the milestone gathering of his remaining parent's birthday. Amidst bluster and genuine loathing, Macleod, and his faithful Sergeant McGrath, must hunt down a killer who seems ready to destroy an entire lineage.

Blood runs thicker than water, every drop!

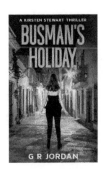

Busman's Holiday (A Kirsten Stewart Thriller #8)

https://grjordan.com/product/busmans-holiday

Kirsten seeks romance and sun on leaving the service. A chance encounter leaves her partner in the middle of a kidnapping. Can Kirsten find her beloved before a terrorist executes him in the name of freedom?

When Kirsten and Craig take a sun drenched holiday in an attempt to cement their love, little do they suspect their quaint destination will become part of a country's nightmare. The black hand rises, murdering a local mayor, and takes Craig hostage, forcing Kirsten to become a merciless rescuer once again. With no back-up, in a land she doesn't understand, the Service's black sheep must curry favours and avoid the local police as she brings down a country's dark underbelly.

How dark your passions when your soul is uneasy!

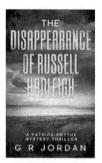

The Disappearance of Russell Hadleigh (Patrick Smythe Book 1)

https://grjordan.com/product/the-disappearance-of-russell-hadleigh

A retired judge fails to meet his golf partner. His wife calls for help while running a fantasy play ring. When Russians start co-opting into a fairly-traded clothing brand, can Paddy untangle the strands before the bodies start littering the golf course?

In his first full novel, Patrick Smythe, the single-armed former policeman, must infiltrate the golfing social scene to discover the fate of his client's husband. Assisted by a young starlet of the greens, Paddy tries to understand just who bears a grudge and who likes to play in the rough, culminating in a high stakes showdown where lives are hanging by the reaction of a moment. If you love pacey action, suspicious motives and devious characters, then Paddy Smythe operates amongst your kind of people.

Love is a matter of taste but money always demands more of its suitor.

Surface Tensions (Island Adventures Book 1)
https://grjordan.com/product/surface-tensions
Mermaids sighted near a Scottish island. A town exploding in anger and distrust. And Donald's got to get the sexiest fish in town, back in the water.

"Surface Tensions" is the first story in a series of Island adventures from the pen of G R Jordan. If you love comic moments, cosy adventures and light fantasy action, then you'll love these tales with a twist. Get the book that amazon readers said, "perfectly captures life in the Scottish Hebrides" and that explores "human nature at its best and worst".

Something's stirring the water!

Corpse Reviver (A Contessa Munroe Mystery #1)

https://grjordan.com/product/corspe-reviver

A widowed Contessa flees to the northern waters in search of adventure. An entrepreneur dies on an ice pack excursion. But when the victim starts moonlighting from his locked cabin, can the Contessa uncover the true mystery of his death?

Catriona Cullodena Munroe, widow of the late Count de Los Palermo, has fled the family home, avoiding the scramble for title and land. As she searches for the life she always wanted, the Contessa, in the company of the autistic and rejected Tiff, must solve the mystery of a man who just won't let his business go.

Corpse Reviver is the first murder mystery involving the formidable and sometimes downright rude lady of leisure and her straight talking niece. Bonded by blood, and thrown together by fate, join this pair of thrill seekers as they realise that flirting with danger brings a price to pay.

Lightning Source UK Ltd.
Milton Keynes UK
UKHW010838010822
406672UK00001B/240